Usborne
Illustrated
Stories for
Children

Usborne
Illustrated
Stories for
Children

CONTENTS

The Princess
and the Pea

Once upon a time there was a prince
who wanted to marry a princess. But
he didn't want just any old princess.

He wanted a real one.

Not one of the local princesses would do. "What's the matter with them, Patrick?" cried his father, the king. "I'm running out of princesses to show you."

"I can't be sure they're real," sighed Prince Patrick. "I'll have to find one for myself."

"You must do whatever you want, darling," said the queen, who spoiled him rotten. "Nothing but the best for my princey-wincey."

MOTHER!

The next day Prince Patrick set out to travel the world, in search of a real princess.

Errrr... I think my arm's stuck.

He took with him twelve suitcases, ten pairs of shoes, a spare crown and his cousin, Fred.

They hadn't gone far when they heard
a loud sneeze from under the seat.
 "Who's there?" shouted the prince.
A small figure crept out.

It's Peg!

"Aren't you the palace maid?"
said Prince Patrick.

Peg nodded.

"Well, what are you doing here?"
the prince asked.

"I want to see the world," said Peg.
"I've been at the palace all my life – ever
since I was left on the doorstep as a baby."

She blushed. "And Cook's furious
because I burned the pudding," she added.

"Well you can't come with us," said Fred. "This is a boys-only adventure. You'll get scared and want to go home."

No I won't! I'm as brave as you.

"We're not turning back now," said Prince Patrick. "She'll have to join us."

Peg grinned at Fred.

"OK," Prince Patrick went on. "First stop, the wicked witch's hut."

"You're joking?" cried Fred in alarm.

She'll eat us ALIVE!

Prince Patrick shook his head. "The witch will know how to find a real princess. She's my best hope..."

"Now Peg," said Prince Patrick, "this could
be dangerous. You stay in the coach.
Fred and I will meet the witch."

The prince knocked three
times on the witch's door...
There was no answer.

"Looks like no one's in. We'll have to go,"
said Fred, who was already backing away.

"She must be in," said the prince, and he bent down to peer through the keyhole.

A large green eye was staring at him. Prince Patrick jumped back and landed bottom-first in a patch of mud.

A short plump woman opened the door,
chuckling to herself. "Did I scare you?
I was just checking who you were.
You can't be too careful these days."

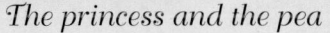

Fred was amazed. "Are you the witch?"
he asked. "You're not scary at all."
The witch looked rather upset. "I try my best,"
she sighed. "I grew three new warts last week."

"Come inside," she added. "I'm just cooking some tasty soup for lunch."

Subthig REALLY sbells in here.

"We're not hungry," said Prince Patrick quickly. "I've come to ask for your help. I want to know how to find a real princess."

"Real princesses are very rare," said the witch, "and it's hard to spot a fake one. But there is a test you can do."

Hmmm... Let me see...

"A real princess must have... boiled brains, rotten beans and cat spit."

"What?" cried the prince.

"Oh sorry, that's a recipe for soup. This is it..."

The real princess test

[A] real princess must possess...

1. Politeness to one and all

2. Kindness to rich and poor

3. Very sensitive skin

"Sensitive skin?" Prince Patrick asked, looking confused.

"A real princess," explained the witch, "has such tender skin that she could feel a pea under twenty mattresses."

"Thank you," said the prince. "You've been very helpful." He turned to the door.

"Oh do stay for lunch," pleaded the witch. "My soup's almost ready. And bring in that poor girl from outside."

No... really, thanks!

Urrgh!! I can't eat THAT!

They were stuck in the witch's hut until the cauldron was empty.

"I feel sick," groaned Peg on the way back to the coach.

"Well, you shouldn't have had three bowls then," said Fred.

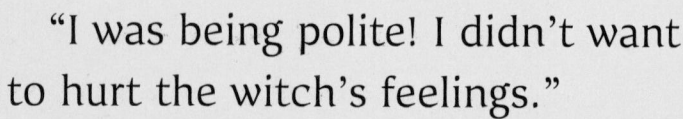

"I was being polite! I didn't want to hurt the witch's feelings."

"That was very kind of you, Peg," said Prince Patrick, smiling at her.

"Where are we going now?" asked Fred.

"Now I have the witch's test, I can finally find a real princess," said the prince. "We're off to meet Princess Prunella. Check the map, Fred."

Princess Prunella was very excited to see the prince. "You must come and stay in my castle," she cried. She raced over the bridge, dragging Prince Patrick with her.

"Hurry! Hurry!" she called
to her servants. "I want you to
prepare the best bedchambers
for the prince and Fred."

"Excuse me," said Peg, struggling with all the luggage. "Where am I to sleep?"

And who are YOU?

I'm a maid.

"Maids belong in the attic," replied the princess, haughtily. "There might be a few mice there, but I'm sure you'll cope."

Peg went to her room. It was cold and damp. She could hear mice scuttling about, squeaking.

The prince can't marry her...

Meanwhile, Fred and the prince were in the grand dining room with Princess Prunella.

"You're being very kind," said Prince Patrick, "but what about Peg? Is she eating in the kitchen?"

The princess looked shocked. "Your beastly little maid? You can't expect me to bother with her."

She can eat the PIG SLOPS if she's hungry.

"I'm afraid we must leave," said Prince Patrick. "You're not a real princess after all."

"Oh yes I am!" cried Princess Prunella.

"Oh no you're not!" shouted Fred.

"You've failed the first real princess test."

"Real princesses are polite to everyone," explained Prince Patrick, "and you've just been rude to Peg."

"I won't give up!" said Prince Patrick. "There must be a real princess somewhere..."

"According to this map, there's a Princess Pavlova next door. Let's try her," Fred suggested.

Princess Pavlova greeted them all very politely. "What a pleasure to have you here," she said. "Welcome to my castle."

"She's passed the politeness test," thought the prince. "Now what's the next one..."

"Fred!" he cried, "I have a plan. I'm going to dress up as a beggar and see if Princess Pavlova is kind to me."

"Try out your disguise on Peg first," said Fred, "to make sure it works."

Prince Patrick found Peg sitting on a tree stump, about to eat an apple. "I'm a hungry beggar," he said.

Have you any food for me?

"Oh you poor thing!" Peg cried, when she saw him. "Here, have my apple."

Prince Patrick was very pleased with himself. "Excellent! It works," he shouted, throwing off his disguise.

It's YOU!

"What are you doing?" asked Peg. But the prince was already knocking on the castle door, to try the test on Princess Pavlova.

A servant answered.

"Is someone there?" called Princess Pavlova.

"It's a beggar, Your Highness."

"We've got nothing for him," snapped the princess. "Tell him to go away."

And he smells...
POO-EE!

Prince Patrick turned away. "She's not a real princess," he thought. "A real princess is both polite and kind – even to beggars."

"I give up," said the prince, with a sigh. "I'll never be married! I don't think there's a real princess anywhere. We may as well go home."

They got ready for the long journey back to the palace. Everyone was glum, even the horses.

"I bet Cook hasn't forgotten about the pudding I burned," thought Peg.

The coach arrived at the palace just in time. A huge storm was brewing.

Peg was sent straight to the
kitchens in disgrace. "You've got
hundreds of dishes to wash,"
scolded the cook. "They've
been piling up since you left."

Prince Patrick and Fred went to find the king
and queen. Outside, rain began beating against
the windows. Streaks of lightning lit up the sky.

Just then, there was a knock on the door.
"There is a Princess Primrose to see you,
Your Highness," said the footman.

A beautiful princess stepped into the
room. She was wet from the rain and
shaking with cold.
"I'm so sorry to trouble you,"
she said politely, "but my coach
has broken down."

43

"No trouble at all," said Prince Patrick quickly. "Why don't you stay the night at our castle? We'll fix your coach in the morning."

I must give you something in return!

"She acts like a real princess," thought the prince, "but I must be sure."

3. Very sensitive skin

He asked the servants
to prepare Princess Primrose's
bedroom.

"I want twenty mattresses on
the bed," ordered Prince Patrick,
"and a pea at the very bottom."

Peg didn't get to bed that night.
She had to finish washing the dishes.

The next morning, Princess Primrose came down for breakfast, looking refreshed.

"How did you sleep?" asked Prince Patrick.

I slept like a baby.

"I loved all those mattresses," the princess said. "It was the most comfortable bed."

Prince Patrick sighed. "A real princess would have felt that pea," he thought. He waved goodbye to Princess Primrose as soon as breakfast was over. "Another fake one," he said, sadly.

It was Peg's job to clean the princess's bedroom. Slowly, she climbed up the ladder, yawning with each step. "I'll just lie down for a moment," Peg thought, "before I start cleaning up."

Zzzzzzzzzz

In no time at all, she was fast asleep.

An hour later, Peg woke with a start. "Ow!"
she said. "There's something really lumpy in
this bed. I'm getting down."

Oooh! It's a long way down!

But as she leaned over, she knocked
the ladder. It clattered to the ground.
"Drat!" Peg cried. "I'm stuck."

"Help!" she shouted, as loudly as she could, "I'm stuck. Please... HELP!"

Everyone rushed into the bedroom.

"What are you doing up there?" Prince Patrick called.

"I was supposed to be cleaning," said Peg, "but I was so tired I fell asleep."

"And there's something horribly hard in this bed," she added. "I'm covered in bruises."

Prince Patrick knew this could only mean one thing...

"I can't believe it!" cried the prince. "You were polite to the witch, kind to a beggar and now you've felt a pea under twenty mattresses. You must be a real princess!"

He raced up the ladder.
"Peg, will you marry me?"
Peg gasped. "You want to marry
me, a palace maid? Yes please!"

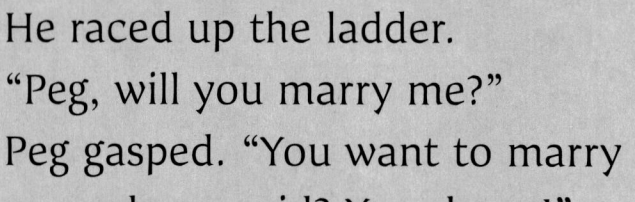

A MAID!?

But a princess
at heart my
dear!

So Prince Patrick finally married his real princess. He put the pea in a glass case in the palace museum for everyone to see.

Ye Royal Pea

It may still be there today...

The ghostly galleon

Harmony lived with her mother at
the very bottom of the ocean.

They were so poor they could only afford a tiny cave. This was cramped, dark and very cold. It froze their fins and took the shine off their scales.

Harmony tried to keep up their spirits by singing beautiful songs. Her voice was so enchanting that passing fish had to stop and listen.

One day, Harmony's mother woke up shivering all over. She was covered in blue spots and her tongue had turned purple. Harmony rushed to find Dr. Finley.

Say ahh.

Ahh....ah.....ahh....ahh.....aaahhh...

"Your mother is very sick," he whispered to Harmony. "The only cure is polkadot seaweed, taken twice a day for one week."

"Where can I find that?"asked Harmony.

"That's the problem," replied Dr. Finley. "It only grows in the Pirates' Graveyard."

"Oh no," gasped Harmony. "Not that spooky place full of sunken pirate ships?"

"I'm afraid so," replied the doctor.

"They say it's haunted by the ghost of Gingerbeard," said Harmony with a shiver. "He was the fiercest pirate to sail the Seven Seas."

The thought of visiting the graveyard filled
Harmony with fear, but she had no choice.
Minutes later, she was swimming
nervously between the creepy wrecks.

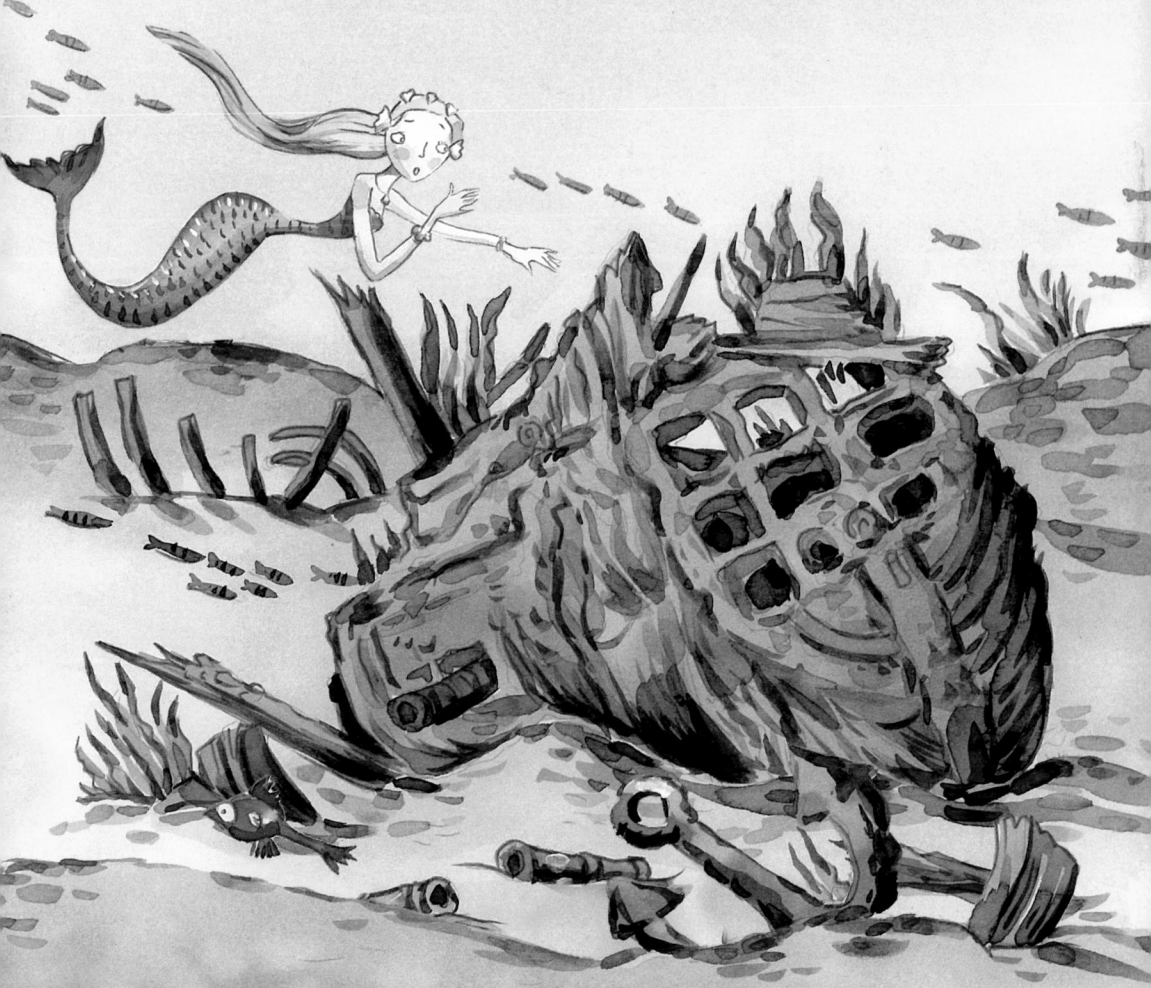

Harmony searched countless ships without luck. She had almost given up hope, when she saw something spotty sticking out of a rusty old cannon.

Suddenly, a terrifying figure appeared from nowhere.

Yahahahaha!

Harmony yelped in fright. It was Gingerbeard's ghost.

"Come to steal my treasure, eh?" snarled the pirate.

"No," cried Harmony. "I just need the polkadot weed to cure my mother."

"I don't believe you," cackled Gingerbeard. He grabbed Harmony roughly and locked her in a cabin.

"No one gets their hands on my gold," screamed the ghost. With that, he shimmered off to patrol the top deck.

Harmony felt terrible. She tried to cheer herself up by singing, but all her songs came out sounding sad.

Harmony's lovely voice floated around Gingerbeard's ship. No matter where he went, the pirate could hear her.

However hard he tried, Gingerbeard couldn't drag himself away from the mermaid's tragic tunes.

As each day passed, he began to feel as sorry for Harmony as a tough old pirate can.

After a week of the singing, Gingerbeard
had had enough.

"I can't take any more!" he sobbed. "Please
just go home and take this chest with you."

Harmony swam home as fast as
she could and opened the chest.
Polkadot weed floated out,
along with handfuls of coins.

Harmony's mother was cured and,
thanks to Gingerbeard's gold, they
moved into a warm and cosy new cave.

Victor saves the village

Victor made barrels, the best barrels in the country.

He made the best barrels because he used the best wood. He hunted hard to find the tallest, straightest trees.

He was always looking out for the perfect tree. So he didn't always watch where he was going. One day, he tripped and fell...

Help!

...into a cave.

Try as he might...

Almost there!

Aaaaaargh!

...Victor couldn't climb out of the cave.

Suddenly, he heard a deep growl.
There was something behind him!
Victor looked. He wished he hadn't.

Sshluurp!

"Please don't eat me!" Victor begged.

"We won't," said one of the dragons. "Not yet. We're going to sleep. Wake us up in the spring."

Victor was stuck. Soon, he was bored as well.

There was nothing he could do.

He had to wait until spring.

All he had to eat and drink were grass and water. After a while, he was no longer as round as a barrel. He was as thin as a twig.

Finally, the dragons awoke.

"We can't eat you!" said one. "You're skin and bone."

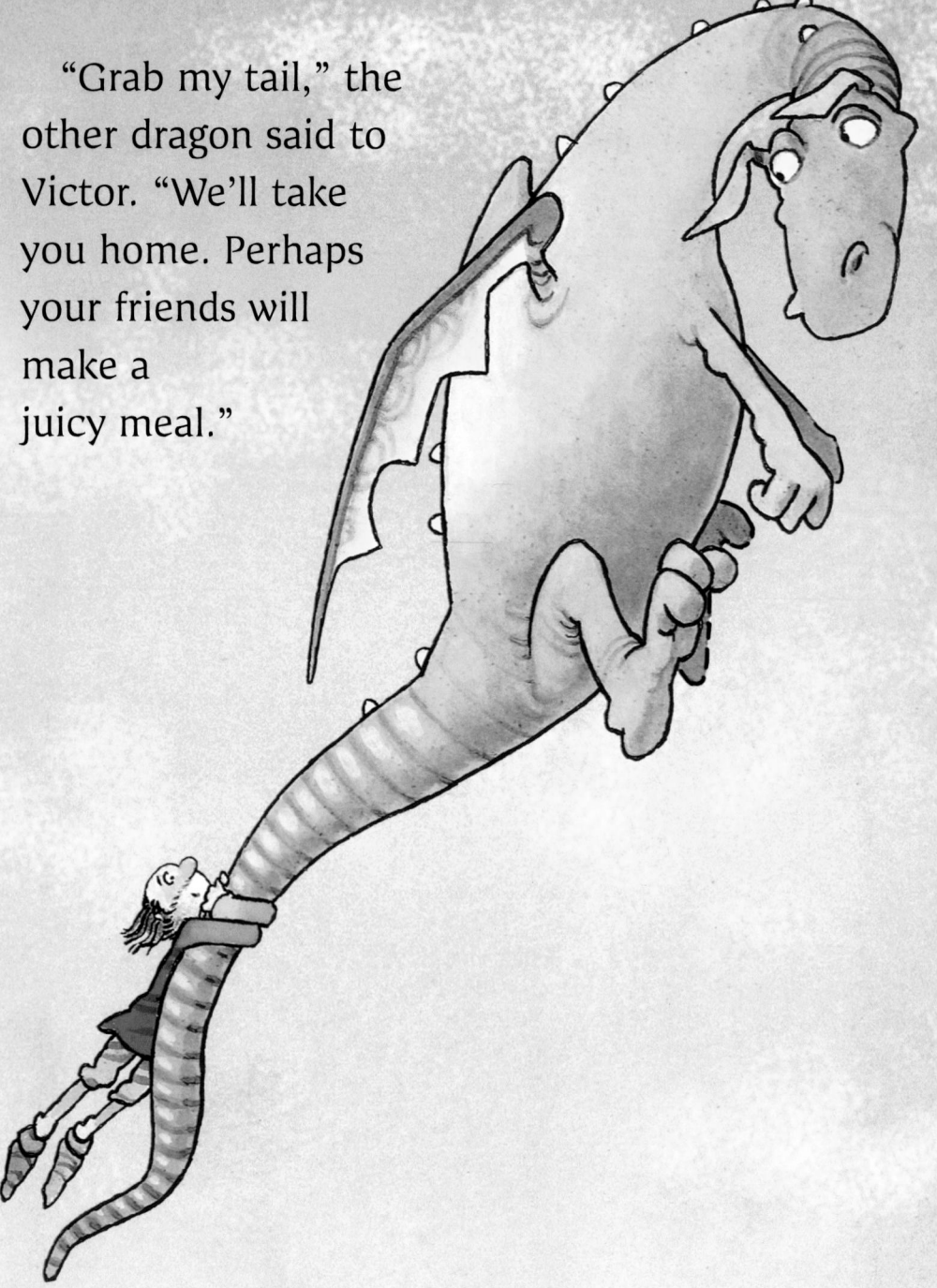

"Grab my tail," the other dragon said to Victor. "We'll take you home. Perhaps your friends will make a juicy meal."

The villagers were amazed to see Victor after so long, and they were terrified to see the dragons.

But before the dragons could bite anyone, Victor invited them to a huge feast.

Victor and the dragons ate for a week.
The dragons enjoyed the food so much, they
decided they would never eat people again.

The villagers were very pleased to hear it. They put up a statue of Victor in the market square.

Now, everyone who visits knows how Victor saved the village from two hungry dragons.

Now he always looks where he's going!

The doll's house

Amy and Tina loved Cherry Tree Cottage.
"It's the prettiest doll's house ever," said Tina.

"And Molly's the best doll owner," Amy added. "We're so lucky to live here."

"You may feel lucky," said Cordelia. "I don't!" Cordelia was a beautiful doll and she knew it.

She had golden curls tied up with a shiny clip and a dress that sparkled with sequins.

"I don't belong here," said Cordelia. "I should be in a doll's palace. Not stuck in this stuffy, boring cottage."

"It's boring because you never do anything,"
said Amy. "You never
help clean or tidy."

"I have more important things to do,"
snapped Cordelia. "Like brushing my hair."

"Please stop fighting," said Tina.
And they had to, as just then they
heard Molly.

RUN!

The dolls rushed back to where Molly had
left them and stayed as still as they could.

"It's a sunny day," Molly told them, "so I'm taking you all on a picnic."

She carefully picked up the dolls and put them in her basket.

"Oh dear," sighed Cordelia, as Molly set them down on an old rug.

"I hope my dress doesn't get dirty."

"Look at your sequins and your clip," Tina whispered, to cheer her up. "They're sparkling in the sun."

But far above in the sky, a magpie had spotted Cordelia too. Like all magpies, he loved collecting sparkly things.

The next moment, he
swooped down and snatched
Cordelia up in his claws.

HEY!
Let me GO!

Cordelia screamed, but the magpie didn't
stop. He flew on and on, higher and higher.

At last they came to a tall tree. The magpie dropped Cordelia into his spiky nest.

"Take me back this second," ordered Cordelia.

The magpie shook his head.
"You're mine now," he said, then
flew away on his bright, glossy wings.

"Oh!" cried Cordelia. "This is horrible."
She spent all day in the nest, feeling
lonelier and lonelier. "Please help me,"
she called to a passing magpie.

Oh no,
I'm ruined!

"Only if you give me your shiny clip,"
said the magpie.

"I'll give you anything you want," sobbed Cordelia. "Just take me home."

At Cherry Tree Cottage, Molly was putting Amy and Tina to bed. "I'll never see Cordelia again," she thought, sadly.

Suddenly, there was a shout.

"Molly!" called her mother. "Look who
I found by the back door!"

There, in the palm of her hand, sat
Cordelia. Her curls were ragged and
wild and her dress was dirty and torn.

"Cordelia!" cried Molly, carefully tucking her into bed. "I can't believe you're back."

"Nor can I," said Amy, once Molly had left. "I thought you hated Cherry Tree Cottage."

"It's no palace," Cordelia said, "but it's much better than a bird's nest. Anyway," she added sadly, "I've lost my sparkle now."

"Never mind," said Amy. "At least you won't be stolen by a magpie again."

Attack of the swamp monster

Tom Smudge loved to listen to his Grandpa
Jess tell creepy stories about the old days.

"Did I ever tell you about the swamp
monster?" asked the old man one afternoon.

"No," gulped Tom nervously.

"It happened years ago," began Grandpa Jess. "I was a farmhand on Roy's ranch, when one of the cows went missing."

"I searched all day with no luck. As night fell, I spotted a muddy trail leading to the middle of the swamp..."

"What happened next?" asked Tom, with a shiver.

"A terrible, slithering sound filled the air, and I found myself face to face with a horrible, hideous..."

Tom, stop bothering your grandpa!

Mrs. Smudge suddenly burst into the room waving a piece of paper at Tom.

"I need you to go to the store and get these things!" she said.

"Can't I hear the end of Grandpa's story first?" begged Tom.

Grocery list

Soap for Grandpa

2 large bottles of bubble bath

Lots of broccoli

Small cabbage

Peas

"No. Now, off you go," said Mrs. Smudge. "And hurry back," she added. "You haven't had a bath yet."

Tom groaned. He hated baths.

He was trudging back from the store when his friends asked him to play football. Thinking of the waiting bath, Tom quickly agreed.

By the time the game ended, it was almost dark. Tom decided to take a shortcut home across the swamp.

He'd only been walking for a minute, when he heard a sinister, squelching sound. Green stalks seemed to be curling around him.

These weeds are very thick!

But they weren't weeds that
Tom could feel tightening
around his ankles...

Dinner time!

Aaaaargh!
The swamp monster!
Heeeelp!

Tom struggled in the slimy creature's grasp. The more he squirmed, the tighter the monster squeezed.

100

Tom wished he'd never stopped to play football.

The monster dragged him closer to its huge, slimy, smelly mouth.

Suddenly there was a crack. The monster had smashed the bottles in Tom's bag.

In seconds, the murky swamp water became a mass of sweet-smelling bubbles.

The monster choked and spluttered on the foamy water. Tom slipped from its grasp. They were both getting the bath of their lives.

By now, several people had heard Tom's shouts and come to help. They took one look at the new, squeaky-clean monster and burst out laughing.

The monster was so embarrassed, it swam off and was never seen again.

As for Tom, he had the best reward ever. He didn't need a bath for a week.

The story of Shiverham Hall

Shiverham Hall

Have a frightful stay, madam!

Shiverham Hall was a hotel with a difference.
All the guests were dead.

Ghosts came from the spirit world to be greeted by Shiverham's spooky staff.

There were twenty-two ice-cold bedrooms...

Aaaahh, l..l..lovely.

a poltergeist-powered jacuzzi...

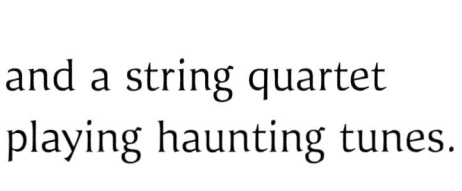

and a string quartet playing haunting tunes.

No living soul dared visit the hotel. It was far too creepy. The ghosts were left in peace.

Then, one afternoon, the hotel's deathly hush was shattered.

Most of the ghosts were napping. Mr. Quiver, the hotel manager, had come down for a glass of water.

Suddenly, a round-faced man flung open the front door and strode up to the reception desk.

"This is just what I've been looking for," he boomed.

A tall, thin man scuttled in after him.

"Um, are you sure, Mr. Slate?" he asked nervously.

"Of course I'm sure, Simkins," barked Slate. "This will make the perfect site for my new hotel. I've had it all designed."

Slate proudly spread out a large plan in front of his assistant. Behind them, Mr. Quiver sneaked up to get a better look.

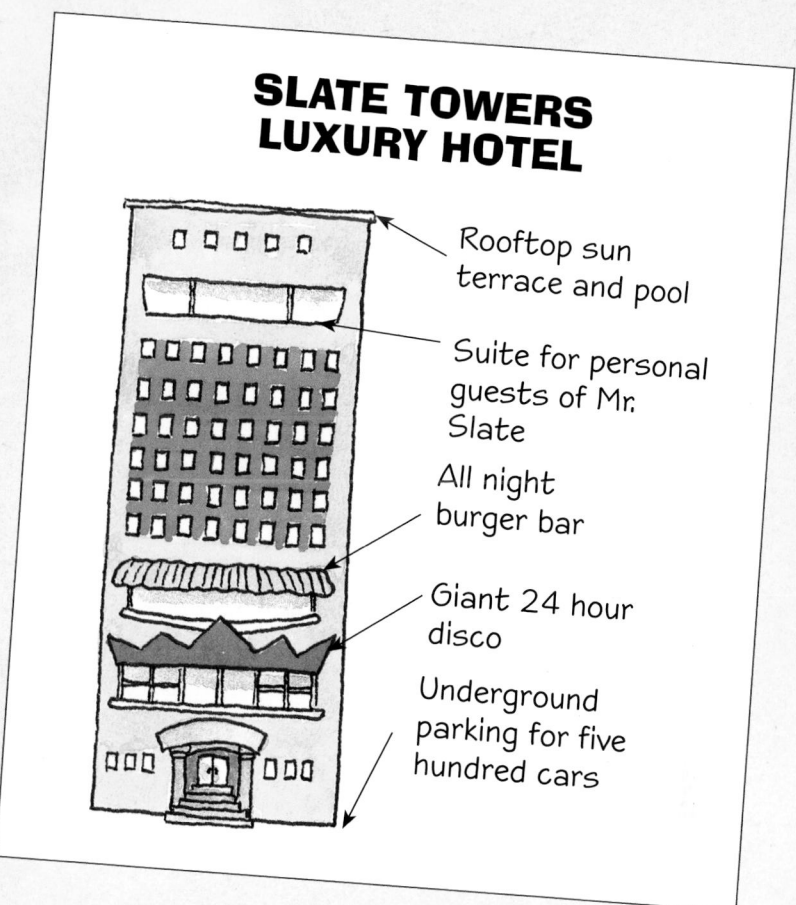

SLATE TOWERS LUXURY HOTEL

Rooftop sun terrace and pool

Suite for personal guests of Mr. Slate

All night burger bar

Giant 24 hour disco

Underground parking for five hundred cars

Mr. Quiver was horrified.

"I'll have this place demolished in no time," Slate went on. "But perhaps I'll look around and see if there's anything worth saving first."

"Don't be too long," gulped Simkins. "They say the place is haunted."

"Ridiculous!" cried Slate. "Ghosts don't exist. And I'll stay the night to prove it."

"We don't exist, eh?" thought Mr. Quiver, as he floated upstairs.

Minutes later, he gathered the hotel staff together. No one was happy about Slate's plans.

"We'll never get any peace in his noisy new hotel," wailed Charlie the waiter.

"And where will our ghostly guests go?" asked Elsie the maid.

"Slate will have to be frightened off," said Mr. Quiver. "As soon as it gets dark, we'll start haunting."

Slate was climbing the rickety stairs to bed, when Mr. Quiver appeared in front of him.

Wooaaahhh! Be gone from Shiverham Hall!

Slate looked a little surprised. But then he shrugged. "Out of my way, potato head!" he shouted.

Mr. Quiver had never been so insulted in his life. Or his death.

But the ghosts weren't finished yet. As Slate brushed his teeth, Igor the porter popped up through the plughole.

Another stupid spook!

Yee haa haaa haaa!

The staff didn't give up. That night, Slate was visited by a stream of ghosts...

Elsie brought the bed sheets to life.

Charlie rattled a ghostly tea tray next to Slate's pillow.

Cora the cook sent possessed pots flying through the air.

Even the hotel guests tried to put the shivers up the unwelcome visitor.

Sir Gauntlet showed off his battle scars.

Lord Doublet lost his head.

And Miss Gauntly, the wailing lady, moaned the entire night.

But none of them could raise a single goosebump.

Next morning, Mr. Quiver listened in on Slate's meeting with Simkins.

"You were right," said Slate. "This place *is* full of ghosts."

"R..r..really?" stuttered Simkins, nervously. "So you'll forget your plans?"

"No way!" said Slate. "People will pay even more to stay in a luxury *haunted* hotel. I'll soon have those spooks hard at work. I'll make a fortune!"

Within minutes, the ghosts' tragic tale appeared on the Spirit World Wide Web.

Ghosts' Online Gazette

SO LONG SHIVERHAM!

HISTORIC HOTEL TO BE FLATTENED - STAFF FACE SLAVERY TO SLATE

The staff of Shiverham Hall are to become a 'tourist attraction' in a new hotel built by Percival Slate.

Percival Slate

It looked as if the ghosts' peaceful life was coming to an end. Next day, the staff watched from the shadows as Slate dreamed of what was to come.

Suddenly, a spooky figure appeared from nowhere.

"Yoo hoo!" she cried.

"Aha!" said Slate. "Another spook, and a very ugly one."

"Don't you recognize me Percy?" said the ghost. "It's me, your Great Aunt Mabel!"

Slate's ghostly aunt planted a slobbery wet kiss on his cheek. Slate's face turned bright red.

"I read all about you on The Ghosts' Gazette website," said Mabel. "So I've decided to come and live in your lovely new hotel."

Let Auntie give you
a nice big KISS!

Live here?
B..b..but...

"I'll look after you, Percy," cried Mabel. "I'll feed you up on my special cabbage soup and I'll make sure you get a bath and a big kiss every bedtime!"

Slate had been terrified of his aunt when she was alive. Now she was even scarier.

"I've ch..changed my mind," he stammered, tore up his plans, and ran.

All the ghosts cheered. Mr. Quiver approached Great Aunt Mabel and bowed.

"Thank you, madam," he said. "Please stay as our guest for as long as you want – for free."

The Masked Pirate

Sam Sardine had always wanted to be a sailor.

He was desperate to travel the Seven Seas and do battle with bloodthirsty pirates.

As soon as he was old enough, he joined Captain Winkle's ship as a cabin boy.

But Sam soon found that life on board ship wasn't as exciting as he'd thought.

He spent all day...

mopping the decks...

peeling potatoes...

...and washing the sailors' smelly socks.

124

Finally, he'd had enough. He went to the captain and asked for a proper sailor's job.

Captain Winkle thought Sam was rather rude. But he decided to put him to the test.

"All right," he said. "Let's see you sail the ship into port!"

Sam's chest swelled with pride as he took the wheel.

But steering a ship wasn't as easy as it looked.

Luckily, the ship wasn't too badly damaged.
Sam begged for one more chance.

"Very well," said Captain Winkle, at last.
"You can guard the ship's treasure."

That night, while the rest of the sailors snored in their bunks, Sam sat guard.

But he was exhausted after his hard day's work. Soon, he was fast asleep as well.

Hours later, Sam was woken from his dreams by a wicked laugh.

He rushed up on deck, to see the dreaded Masked Pirate sailing off with Captain Winkle's treasure.

Sam felt terrible. What would the captain say? He didn't have to wait long to find out.

When Captain Winkle had calmed down, he offered a reward to whoever could track down the thief or his treasure.

But, as the pirate always wore a mask, no one knew what he looked like. Suddenly, Sam had an idea. "I'll find the pirate *and* your treasure," he said.

Captain Winkle didn't have much confidence in his cabin boy, but no one else had a plan.

That evening, Sam went to the Spyglass Inn, where the local pirates spent the night.

132

At breakfast next morning, Sam said in a loud voice, "I heard the Masked Pirate talking in his sleep last night. He described the exact spot where he hides his treasure!"

One particular pirate sitting in a corner began to look worried. Sam's plan was working.

"Now I know where the treasure is, I'm going to get it for myself!" Sam went on.

Hearing this, the pirate rushed out of the inn. Sam followed close behind.

The pirate jumped into a boat and rowed to an island just off the coast.

Sam ran to Captain Winkle, yelling,
"Follow that pirate!"

When they arrived
on the island,
they found the
pirate hurriedly
digging up a
treasure chest.

The captain recognized it at once. It was *his* treasure chest. Taking a flying leap, he landed on the pirate.

"Take my ship and fetch help, Sam my boy!" he roared.

"You trust me to sail?" cried Sam. He grinned from ear to ear. "Aye aye, Captain!" he said.

The Nutcracker

A nutcracker is a wooden or metal tool for cracking nutshells. When this story was written, nuts were a special Christmas treat. Some nutcrackers were even shaped like dolls and given as presents.

This is the tale of a rather
unusual nutcracker doll...

A soft, fluffy layer of snow covered
Clara's house on Christmas Eve.

Inside, a party was in full swing, but one very special guest hadn't arrived. Clara watched for him at the window.

Suddenly, there was a loud
knock on the door.
   "He's here!" she cried, dancing
over and flinging open the door.

It was Clara's godfather. She gave him a big hug.

"What a warm welcome on such a chilly night!" he said, with a chuckle.

Clara loved her godfather's visits. Something magical always happened when he was around.

"I have a very special present for you this year," he told Clara, as he placed a package under the tree.

That night, Clara couldn't sleep. She lay in bed thinking about her present. "It can't hurt if I just have a little peek," she thought.

Finally, Clara tiptoed downstairs. She soon found the present, tied up with a big red bow. On the ribbon there was a tag with a message.

Merry Christmas Clara.
I hope this protects you...
With love from your
godfather x

"I wonder what Godfather means," thought Clara.

Slowly, Clara untied the bow and
folded back a corner of the paper...
    Inside, she found a wooden nutcracker
doll, dressed like a soldier.

Just then, the clock struck midnight. Clara gave an enormous yawn. In a few minutes, she was fast asleep under the tree.

Clara woke up with a start, feeling very confused. She couldn't remember where she was and her doll had vanished.

She looked around and saw she was under the Christmas tree... and it seemed to be growing.

What's happening?

But the tree wasn't growing – she was shrinking. Soon, she was as small as a mouse.

Out of the corner of her eye, Clara thought she saw something leaping around. Frightened, she darted behind a present...

...and heard the tree rustle behind her. Clara spun around.

"Don't be afraid, Clara. I won't hurt you,"
said a friendly voice. Clara was astonished.

Her doll had come to life!
"I'm the Nutcracker Prince," he said, with a
bow, "and I'm here to protect you. The kitchen
mice are plotting to kidnap you."

The prince pulled out a whistle and gave a shrill blow. At once, the lid of the toy box flew open and a long line of toy soldiers marched out.

Standing in rows, they saluted the prince.
"Attention!" he cried. "Clara needs our help.
Prepare yourselves for battle, men."

Wheel
out the
cannons!

Mice began to appear in the shadows. Slowly, they crept closer. Clara hid behind the prince.

"Steady, men... steady," he shouted. "Wait for the signal – and FIRE!"

Huge lumps of cheese flew from the cannons and struck down several mice. Some lumps landed in the corners and the other mice scampered after them.

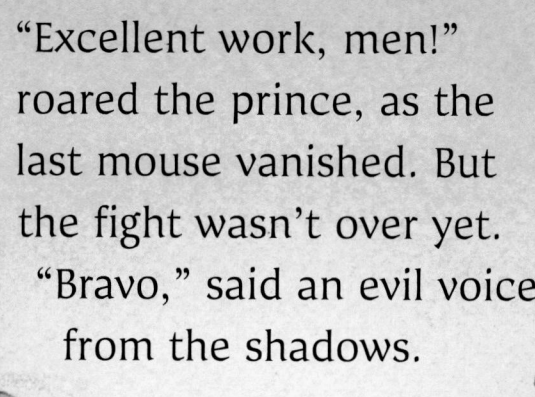

"Excellent work, men!"
roared the prince, as the
last mouse vanished. But
the fight wasn't over yet.
"Bravo," said an evil voice
from the shadows.

A mouse wearing a
crown and an eye
patch appeared.

"That's the Mouse King," the
prince whispered to Clara.
"Is cheese the best you can do?"
jeered the king. "It'll take more than that
to beat me! Now hand over the girl."

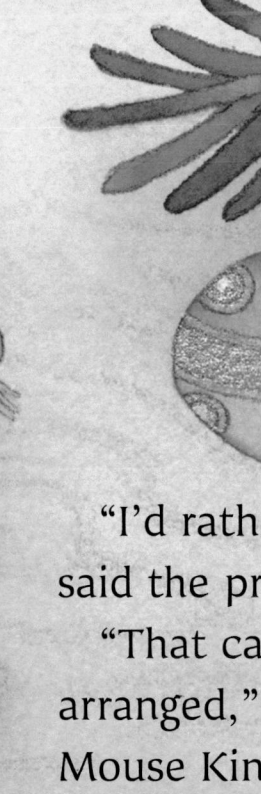

"I'd rather die!"
said the prince.
"That can be
arranged," the
Mouse King sneered.

Soon, the prince and the Mouse King were locked in battle. Their swords clanged as they danced around the room.

Then disaster struck. The prince tripped on a lump of cheese and sprawled on the floor. Seizing his chance, the Mouse King put his sword to the prince's neck.

Well, well, well...

"I'm going to enjoy this," he said, laughing.

As the Mouse King pulled back his
sword, Clara whipped off her shoe and
threw it as hard as she could at his
head. He fell in a heap on the floor
– knocked out cold.

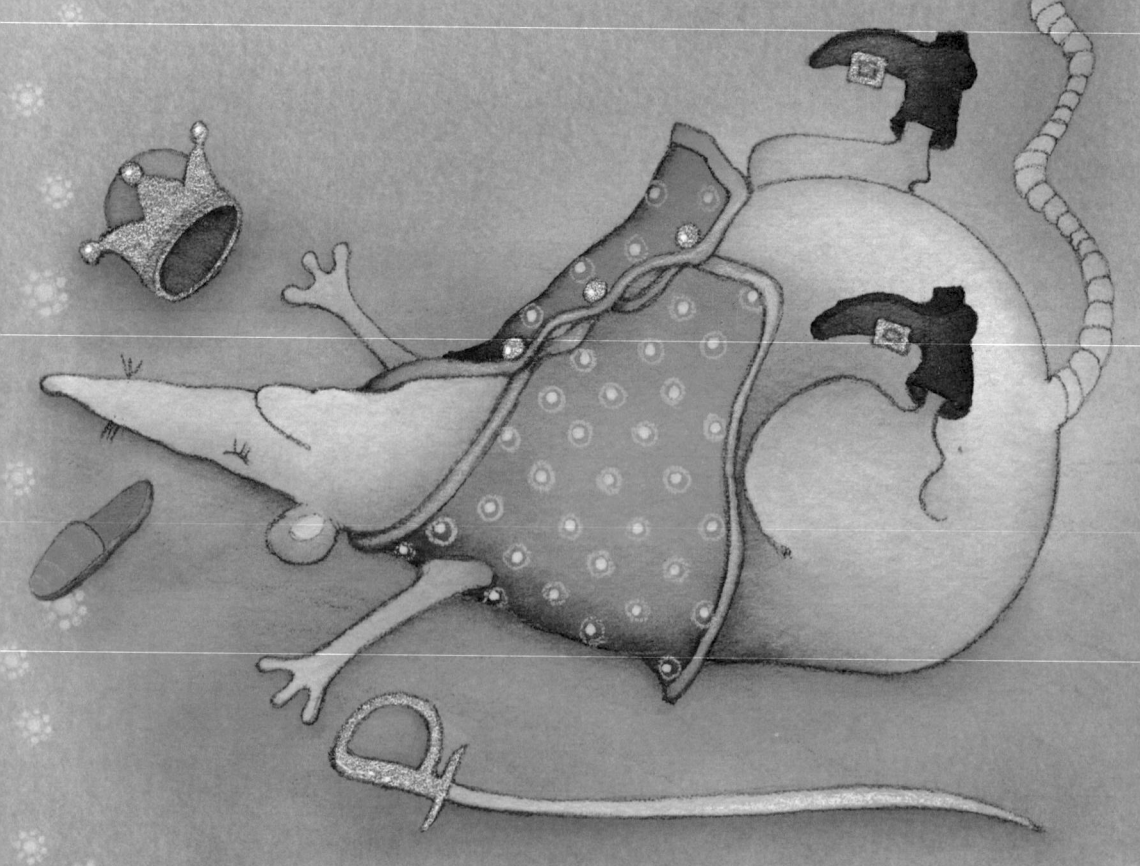

Clara rushed over to the prince.
"Are you alright?" she cried.
"Yes – thanks to you," he said.
"We must celebrate," he added,
as Clara helped him up.
"I know just the place."

The prince led Clara to a golden sleigh behind the Christmas tree and helped her aboard.

"Off we go, boys!" the prince called to his four reindeer.

As they
gathered speed,
the sleigh started
to rise up into the air.
They rode out through an
open window and into the night.

After some time, they came to a forest covered with crisp white snow.

"We're nearly at our first stop," the prince announced. "Hold on, we're going down!"

The snow crunched under the reindeer's feet as they landed.

Just then, a beautiful lady dressed in sparkling white appeared among the trees.

"Clara, I'd like you to meet my good friend, the Ice Queen," said the prince.

"What a lovely surprise!" exclaimed the queen.

The queen led them to her icy palace,
which glistened in the moonlight.

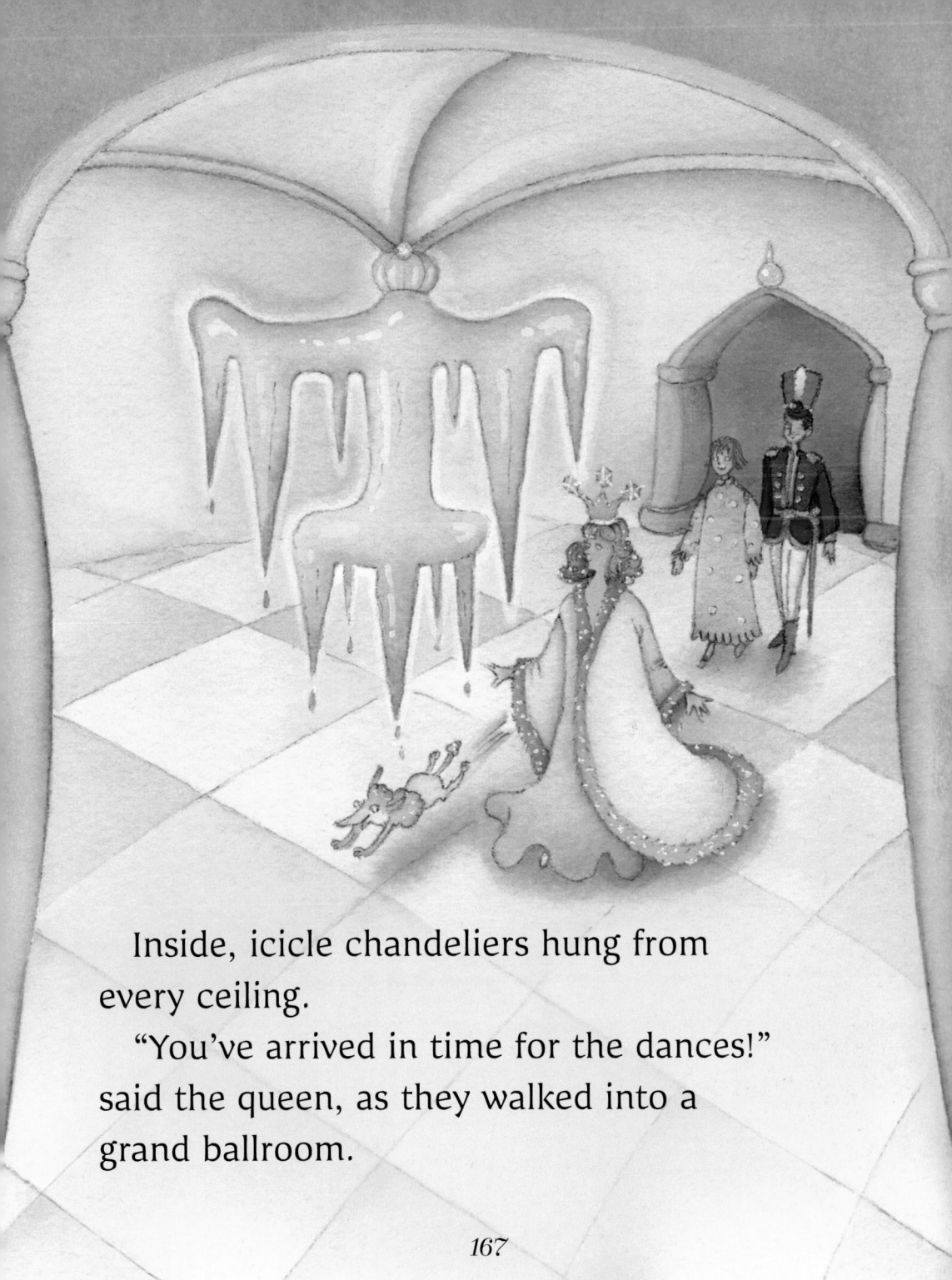

Inside, icicle chandeliers hung from every ceiling.

"You've arrived in time for the dances!" said the queen, as they walked into a grand ballroom.

A piano began to play and eight ballerinas dressed in silver and white twirled into the middle of the room. They twinkled like snowflakes as they spun around.

"I'll always remember this," whispered Clara to the prince, as the music came to an end.

After a game of catch with the palace poodle, it was time to leave.

"Do we really have to go?" sighed Clara.

"Yes, we really do," said the prince. "There's someone else I want you to meet and we don't have much time."

Clara gasped when they reached their next stop. The trees were bursting with marshmallow blossoms, and lollipop flowers sprouted from the ground.

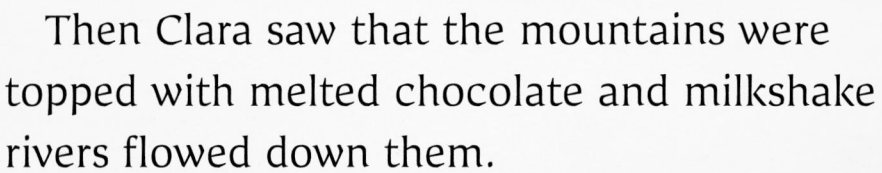

Then Clara saw that the mountains were topped with melted chocolate and milkshake rivers flowed down them.

"Where are we?" she asked, amazed.

"The Land of Sweets!" the prince replied. Before them stood a huge marzipan castle, decorated with all kinds of treats.

Lifting Clara from the sleigh, he set her down on the palace steps and a fanfare of trumpets rang out. At the top, the doors opened and a fairy appeared, dressed from head to toe in pink.

"Clara, this is the Sugarplum Fairy," said the prince. "She rules over the Land of Sweets."

"I hope you have a sweet tooth," said the Sugarplum Fairy, with a smile.

She led them into a grand hall, where the tables were covered with chocolate cakes, cookies and candy swirls.

"Watch the wobbly chairs," whispered the prince as Clara sat down. "They're made of raspberry mousse!"

Clara ate until she thought she'd pop.

After the feast, a band struck up and dancers from around the world performed for Clara.

First came the dance of chocolate,
and a Spanish pair spun around
to snapping castanets.

Next came the exotic dance
of coffee. A beautiful Arabian
princess danced with smooth,
swirling movements in time
to soft, soothing music.

The third group of dancers had come all the way from China to entertain everyone with their tea dance.

Many more dances followed, each one showing something good to eat or drink.

But the final dance was very different.
A group of ballerinas, all dressed as flowers,
performed a slow waltz for Clara.

Their arms unfolded gracefully like
the petals of a flower, as they weaved
in and out of each other.

"And now I'm afraid it's time for us to go home," said the prince sadly. With a sigh, Clara climbed into the sleigh and waved goodbye to the Sugarplum Fairy.

"Thank you for an amazing evening, Nutcracker Prince," said Clara, with a yawn. She was so tired that she fell asleep on his shoulder.

When Clara woke up, she was back under the Christmas tree and the prince was gone.

Only her doll lay beside her.

"Oh, it was only a dream," she cried. "But it seemed so real."

Just then, Clara spotted the tag that her godfather had attached to her present.

"I hope this protects you," it said.

"I wonder if that means he knew the Nutcracker Prince would rescue me," thought Clara. "Maybe it wasn't just a dream..."

Merry Christmas Clara,
I hope this protects you...
With love from your
godfather x

Jon and the green troll

Once, there was a poor farmer. His wife was dead. He lived with his only son, Jon, near the mountains in Scotland.

In the spring and summer, Jon and his father worked hard in the fields.

This tree just won't **budge!**

In the autumn, they shut up the farm and went down to the sea, to fish.

But, one year, Jon's father felt too old for the trip. "You'll have to go alone," he said to Jon.

Take good care of yourself!

Don't worry, I will!

"Just remember one thing," his father warned. "Don't stop at the big, black rock. That's where the trolls live."

As Jon drove up a rocky mountain path, the sky grew dark. Then a storm blew up. Lightning flashed and thunder growled. "I wish my dad were here," thought Jon.

At last, he saw a big, black rock. "Ah! I can shelter there," he thought.

Jon had forgotten his father's warning. He was just glad to be out of the storm. He sat down outside a cave and unpacked his sack.

Whew!
That journey made
me really hungry!

"Time for supper," he said to himself. He had crusty bread, smelly cheese, an apple and a very big fish. "Delicious!" he said, as he chomped away.

Suddenly, Jon heard a noise coming from inside the cave. He was so scared, he stopped chewing.

He could hear voices – babies' voices! "Wahhh!" they cried. "We're hungry!"

Jon quickly picked up the fish and cut it in half. He threw both halves into the cave. "Here, eat these!" he called.

The crying stopped at once.
"Whew," said Jon. "Thank goodness for that."

He was almost asleep when a giant shadow fell over him. Jon looked up. A troll! A troll was coming for him.

"I smell a man!" said a low, rumbling voice.

Now, Jon remembered his father's warning. But it was too late.

The troll came over to Jon and picked him up. He shook with terror. This was his first fishing trip alone – and he was the one to be caught. "Please, don't eat me!" he begged.

But the troll was gentle. "Don't be scared," she said. "I want to thank you for feeding my children."

The troll took Jon into her cave and looked after him. She even gave him her children's bed. It was lumpy but Jon slept well.

The next morning, after breakfast, the troll waved Jon off.

"Take these magic fishing hooks," she said. "When you reach the sea, look for an old man named Charlie. You must go fishing with him."

"Thank you," said Jon. "I will."

"But only fish near the pointed rock," the troll warned.

Jon did just as the troll had said. He found
Charlie in an old hut by the beach.

"Will you come fishing with me?" asked Jon.

"Are you sure?" asked Charlie. "I'm the
worst fisherman in the world. I never catch
anything!"

Charlie showed Jon his boat. It was full of holes and falling to pieces.

"Don't worry!" said Jon. "I can soon fix that."

He set to work with some tar and planks of wood. Soon, the boat was as good as new.

"Let's row to that pointed rock," Jon said to Charlie. They put worms on the magic hooks, and started to fish. "Hey!" Jon cried, a few seconds later. "I've caught one!"

"So have I!" shouted Charlie.

And another!

And another!

They couldn't believe their luck. The boat
was full of fish!

The other fishermen couldn't believe it either.
"What's your secret?" they asked.

Jon told them to fish near the pointed rock.
But, when they tried, they didn't catch a thing.

Every day for the entire winter, Jon's magic hooks caught hundreds of fish. "They've done it again!" gasped a local fisherman.

"Charlie's lucky at last!" said another, shaking his head in disbelief.

Every day, Jon and Charlie cleaned the fish and hung them up to dry. They had more fish than all the other fishermen put together.

"There's something fishy going on here," one of them grumbled.

When spring came, it was time for Jon to go home. On the way, he visited the troll and gave her half his fish. "I never could have caught them without you," he said.

"Thank you," she said. "One day, you'll have a dream about me. When you do, you must come back to my cave."

Back at home, Jon helped his father on the farm. A year later, he had a dream about the troll – just as she had said. "I have to go and visit someone," he told his dad.

He quickly left for her cave, without telling his father where he was going.

At last, he reached the cave. He peered inside.

"Hello?" he called. "Is anybody home?"

There was no answer.

Jon crept into the cave. It was empty except for two chests. "Are they for me?" Jon wondered. What could be inside?

He put the chests on his cart and took them home. When he opened them, he found piles of treasure and gold. Jon and his father were so rich, they never had to work again. "Hip hip hooray!" they cheered.

Jon never told his father where the money came from.

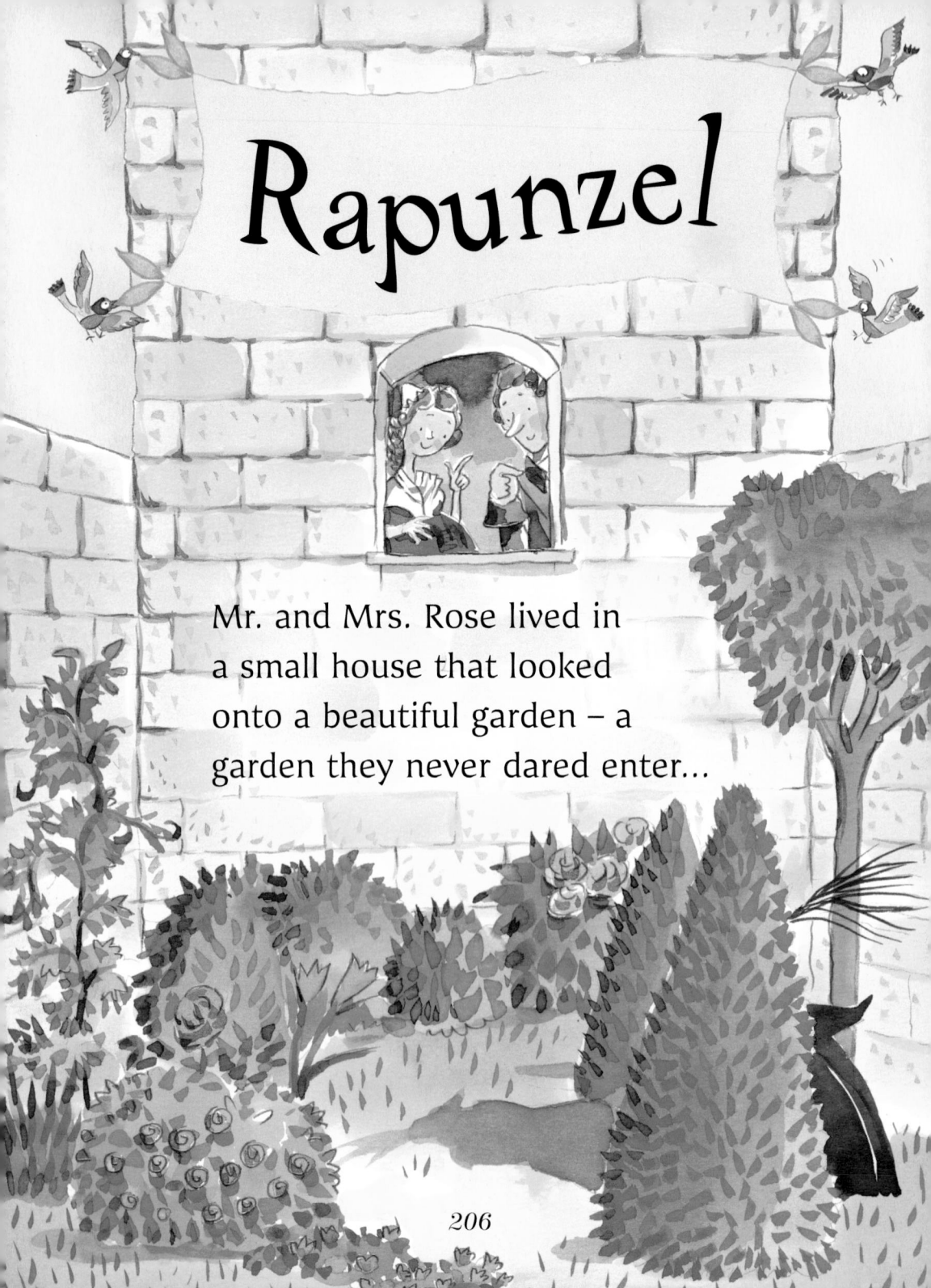

Rapunzel

Mr. and Mrs. Rose lived in
a small house that looked
onto a beautiful garden – a
garden they never dared enter...

...because it belonged to a wicked and powerful witch.

Mrs. Rose would sit by her window and gaze at the garden for hours.

But lately, she had spent a lot of time thinking about food. "Today, I'd like chocolate pudding stuffed with spinach..." she decided.

...and minced frog.

Mr. Rose wasn't surprised. "Ever since you've been pregnant," he said, "you've wanted to eat the oddest things."

"Or perhaps," Mrs. Rose went on, "I'll have bananas, Brussels sprouts and, um, toothpaste. Oh yes, that would be lovely."

"Are you sure?" asked Mr. Rose.

"Yes," Mrs. Rose replied, "I am. Although I still think something might be missing..."

"Wait a moment!" Mrs. Rose cried, pointing to the witch's garden. "That's it."

"What is?"

"That vegetable. Oooh. It looks so green and juicy. I must have it!"

Mr. Rose looked. "Well you can't have it," he said. "I'm not going in that garden. The witch would eat me alive!"

"If I don't have that plant, I'll die," said Mrs. Rose and she began to cry.

210

After three hours of sobbing,
Mr. Rose gave in. That night,
he crept into the witch's garden.

"These vegetables all look the same in the dark," he thought. "How am I meant to know which one she wants?"

So he grabbed the nearest vegetable and raced home.

"You stupid sausage!" cried Mrs. Rose. "You've brought me a turnip."

You'll HAVE to go back again!

Next time, Mr. Rose looked carefully around the garden. "Well, this one has green leaves. It must be right," he thought. But as he pulled it out of the ground, he shuddered. A foul smell had crept up his nose.

He looked up and screamed. The witch
was in front of him. Mr. Rose could smell
her disgusting witchy breath.

"How dare you steal my rapunzel?" the witch
cried. "I'll make you pay for this, you thieving
little pimple!"

"I'll eat you alive," she hissed, a nasty glint in her eye. "I'm sure you'll be very tasty."

"P-p-please don't eat me," begged Mr. Rose.

He was shaking with fear. "I was taking it for my wife. She's about to have a b-b-baby," he stammered.

"Hmm," said the witch, thoughtfully.
"A baby?" She paused for a moment.
"I'll make a deal with you. I won't kill you and
you can have as much rapunzel as you like...

Th-th-thank you,
th-thank you,
thank you.

...but you must give me the baby
as soon as it's born."

Mr. Rose was so terrified, he agreed. He walked slowly home, shaking his head with worry. "Maybe she'll change her mind?" he thought, desperately.

But as soon as his wife gave birth to their daughter, the witch appeared.

"The child is mine," she cried. She gave a wicked grin. "And I shall call her Rapunzel, after the plant you stole. Now, give!"

Mrs. Rose wept and wept. "Don't take my baby," she pleaded.

But the witch would not give in.

She snatched the baby, and vanished.

TOO LATE!
The deal is
done.

Rapunzel lived with the witch for eleven years. She was treated like a slave.

GET ME TEN SLUGS FOR MY SPELL!

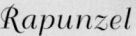

The older she grew, the more beautiful Rapunzel became. She had blue eyes and long golden hair. It flowed from the top of her head...

down her back...

past her feet...

...and all along the ground.

"Rapunzel's getting too pretty," thought the witch. "I'll have to lock her away. I don't want any young men running off with her."

On the morning of Rapunzel's twelfth birthday, the witch woke her early.

"I have a lovely surprise for you," she said. "We're going to the forest for a picnic."

The forest was deep and
dark. It didn't seem a good
choice for a picnic. In the
very middle of the forest
stood a tower.

"I don't like it here,"
Rapunzel said, with
a shudder.

Heh hehe hehe!

"Get used to it," cackled the witch,
"because this is your new home."

The witch cast a spell, and Rapunzel found herself in a small room, at the very top of the tower.

"I can't live here," cried Rapunzel. "There's no way out – no stairs, no door..."

"You don't need to get out," said the witch, "I just need to get in. And I can climb up your hair!"

"Maybe I won't let you," said Rapunzel.

"Then you'll starve," said the witch, with a shrug. "Come on, let's try."

Rapunzel, Rapunzel, let down your hair!

Rapunzel heaved her hair out of the window. Her long locks tumbled down the tower and landed at the witch's feet.

The witch climbed up
Rapunzel's hair...

...and into the tower.

Four years went by. Rapunzel never
saw anyone, except the old witch.
She was very, very bored.

And no one in the world
knew where Rapunzel was.
Until one day...

...a young and handsome prince rode
through the forest. Rapunzel spotted
him from her window.

"Help!" she cried, as loudly as she could. "Please, help me!"

The prince looked up, astonished.

"Don't worry," he called, "I'll save you."
Spurring on his horse, he galloped to the tower. "Prince Hans to the rescue!" he called.

He rode around the tower three times.
"Um, I can't find the door," he said.

"There is no door," Rapunzel
told him. "This is a magic tower.
I'm being kept here by a wicked
witch. You must climb up my hair."

"Well I've never done that before," said Prince Hans. "This is harder than it looks, you know," he added, as he began to climb. "What's your name?" he asked.

"Rapunzel," she replied.

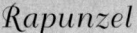

Prince Hans almost fell off her hair, laughing.

"Just what's so funny?" Rapunzel asked haughtily.

"You've got the same name as a vegetable!" said Prince Hans, still chuckling.

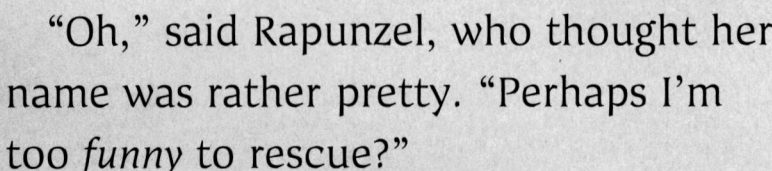

"Oh," said Rapunzel, who thought her name was rather pretty. "Perhaps I'm too *funny* to rescue?"

"Not at all," said Prince Hans, as he reached the top of the tower. "But how am I going to save you?"

"You're the prince," said Rapunzel. "You think of something."

Prince Hans looked around the room thoughtfully and spotted a pair of scissors.

Gosh, I'm brilliant!

"I know!" he cried, "I'll cut off your hair, make a rope and then we can both climb down it."

"You are *not* cutting off my hair," said Rapunzel. "Have you any idea how long it took to grow?"

"Fine," replied Prince Hans, "but you'll have to come up with a better idea, or your hair gets it."

Rapunzel thought quickly. "Visit me every night and bring a ball of silk with you. I'll weave a ladder from it."

"But that'll take ages," said Prince Hans. Rapunzel frowned at him.

"...which isn't a problem," he added quickly.

After that, the prince came every evening. He told Rapunzel about his kingdom. "I live in a beautiful castle," he said. "There are courtyards full of fountains and flowers..."

...and turrets that touch the sky.

As the weeks passed, Rapunzel's ladder grew longer and longer. "Only one more week and I'll be free..." she thought to herself one morning.

"Rapunzel," the witch called from outside, "Rapunzel, let down your hair. I have some food for you."

As the witch climbed up, she pulled and tugged painfully on Rapunzel's hair.

"Ow!" cried Rapunzel.
"Why do you always
tug so much? Prince
Hans never hurts me
when he climbs."

WHAT?!

"Prince Hans?" shouted the witch.
"Who is Prince Hans? You *wicked* girl!
I thought I'd shut you away from the
world, but you've tricked me."

The witch leaped into the tower and quickly grabbed a pair of scissors. She hacked away at Rapunzel's hair until it lay in a heap on the floor.

"I haven't finished," cried the witch. With a powerful spell, she cast Rapunzel into the desert.

Then the witch waited for the prince, a sly smile on her wrinkled face.

Rapunzel, Rapunzel! Let down your hair!

That night, Prince Hans called out to Rapunzel as usual. Her hair came shimmering down.

But when the prince reached the
top of the tower, he gasped in shock.
An ugly old crone stood in her place.
"Where's Rapunzel?" he demanded.

"Rapunzel's gone," said the witch, with a
sinister laugh. "You'll never see her again."

Then the witch leaned out of the tower
and kissed Prince Hans with her slimy lips.
"Yuck!" cried the prince.

It was a magic kiss. Suddenly, the prince's
hands were covered in slime. He lost his grip
and fell to the ground like a stone.

Prince Hans landed smack in a thorn bush. It saved his life, but the sharp thorns blinded him.

Aaargh!
I can't see!

Despite his pain, Prince Hans stood up.
"I may be blind," he shouted to the witch, "but I'll find Rapunzel."
"Never!" she cackled.

Prince Hans wandered for months
seeking Rapunzel. At last, he met
a camel seller who told him
about a girl with golden hair
and blue eyes, living alone
in the middle of the desert.

Prince Hans hired a driver and
the fastest horses he could find.
"Take me to the desert," he said.

Rapunzel watched the carriage arrive in amazement. As Prince Hans stumbled out, she ran to him, put her arms around his neck and wept.

Two of her tears fell into Prince Hans' eyes, and he gasped. "I can see!" he cried.

"Rapunzel," he said, "I never thought I'd say this to a girl named after a vegetable, but will you marry me?"

"Oh yes!" said Rapunzel.

Prince Hans took Rapunzel to his castle. The entire kingdom was invited to their wedding, including Mr. and Mrs. Rose.

Princess Rapunzel and Prince Hans lived
happily together for the rest of their lives
and, in time, had three beautiful children
– Pumpkin, Lettuce and Sprout.

The tale of the haunted TV

One Saturday afternoon, Glen Goggle was watching TV. Suddenly the set made a funny fizzing noise and the screen went black.

Glen's dad called out Mr. Sparks, the
TV repairman.

"You've worn it out, lad," said Mr. Sparks.

"It wasn't my fault!" said Glen.

Mr. Sparks put the television in his van and
returned with a battered-looking replacement.
Glen had never seen such an ancient TV set.

"It's better than nothing," said Mr. Goggle.
Glen's parents had no problems watching
the TV. But the first time that Glen tuned in,
something odd happened. A man in strange
clothes appeared on the screen and burst
into song.

"This isn't Cartoon Club," muttered Glen.

"Welcome, one and all, to the world of Harry Hall!" sang the man on the TV. Harry was a terrible singer. But he was so funny, Glen didn't mind missing the cartoons.

The next time Glen switched on, Harry appeared again. This time he was dressed as a magician.

This show was even funnier than the last. Every trick Harry did went wrong.

Oh dear!

Oops!

Oh no.

The useless magician made Glen laugh so much, he had to turn off the TV to stop his sides from aching.

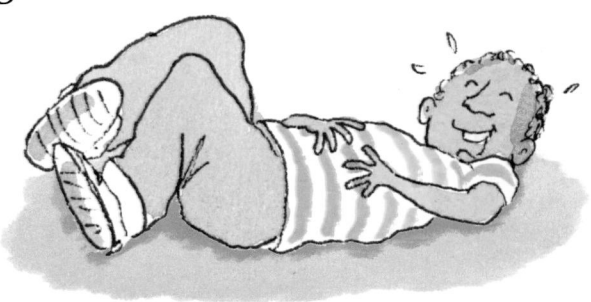

Next day, Harry tried
to dance and kept
tripping over his own feet.
Although Harry was funny,
Glen was starting to miss
the cartoons.

Glen was about to
switch channels, when
Harry fell forward
– right through the
TV screen. Then
he grew to full
size before Glen's
astonished eyes.

"Sorry," panted Harry. "I should have taken more dance lessons when I was alive."

Glen gulped. "You mean, you're a g...g..."

Ghost? That's right!

"I always wanted to be on television," said Harry. "So when I became a ghost, I decided to haunt this set."

"You were very funny," said Glen.

"I didn't mean to be," Harry replied.

"I can't rest easy in the spirit world until I'm a star," he sighed.

Glen felt sorry for Harry. He offered to let him stay if he stopped haunting the TV.

Harry spent the next few days moping in Glen's room.

Then one afternoon, Glen showed him a ticket. "Look where we're going," he said, with a grin.

Come and watch

TALENT TIME

The Top TV Talent Contest
being recorded
Saturday October 4 at 3:00pm
at XYZ TV Studios
BIG CASH PRIZE FOR THE TOP ACT!

Harry was full of excitement. He'd never seen a TV show being made before.

Glen wasn't sure if spooks were allowed in
TV studios. Harry shrank himself down so Glen
could smuggle him inside.

Glen was relieved when he reached his seat
in the audience. Harry peeked out as the lights
dimmed and the show began.

There were singers, dancers and comedians. Glen thought they were great, but Harry did nothing but grumble. "I could do better than that!" he complained.

"Shh!" said Glen, who was getting some funny looks from the woman beside them.

Glen didn't notice the ghost float away. So he got a shock when a full-size Harry suddenly appeared on stage.

Harry pushed the other contestants aside and went into his act.

He sang terrible songs...

he messed up his magic tricks...

and he finished with his clumsy dance routine.

The audience roared with laughter. Harry won first prize as the star of the show. He called Glen on stage to say thank you.

With a big grin on his face, Harry faded away. Glen grinned too. Harry had given him the prize money to buy a brand new TV.

THE PRINCESS AND THE PIG BOY

Once, a poor prince named Sam lived in a tiny castle. All he owned was a beautiful rose tree and a lovely nightingale.

Sam fell in love with a rich princess named Sara. So, he sent her his beautiful tree and the lovely nightingale.

But Sara was not pleased. "A silly tree and a noisy bird?" she said. "Send them back!"

Sam didn't give up. He went to Sara's palace and got a job taking care of the palace pigs.

"They don't smell as sweet as my rose tree," he thought.

But Sam missed his home. He especially missed the lovely songs of his nightingale. So, he made a rattle which played magical tunes.

It's put the pigs to sleep!

Sara was out with her maids when she heard the rattle.

"I want it!" she said.

"It costs one hundred kisses," said Sam.

"Never!" said Sara. But she did want the rattle. "I'll give you ten kisses," she said.

"The price is one hundred," said Sam. Sara had to give in.

Yu..u..ukk!

The king was on his balcony, when he heard giggling. It was coming from the pig sty.

What's going on down there?

The king hurried down. He crept up behind
Sara's maids and looked over their shoulders.
"Hmm, someone's kissing the pig boy,"
he said. Then he realized. "It's Sara!"

The king was very angry. "Princesses don't kiss pig boys!" he shouted. "Both of you must leave at once."

GO AND NEVER COME BACK!

Sam and Sara had to leave the palace.

"I don't even like pigs," said Sara.
"I wish I'd married that poor prince."
Sam quickly changed his clothes
behind a tree. "You can!" he cried.

Sam took Sara to live in his tiny castle.
Sometimes, she even watered the rose tree.

The pesky parrot

It was Charlie Crossbones' first day as a pirate.

He'd spent the last ten years at Pirate School.
Now he was ready to set sail for treasure.

He knew how to...

read a
treasure map...

unlock a chest...

...and do lots of other
piratey things.

What's more, Charlie had been lucky enough to inherit his Grandpa's old pirate ship and all the gear to go with it.

But as Charlie looked at his outfit, he realized something was missing. He didn't have a parrot.

Every pirate needs a parrot.

A moment later, Charlie spotted just what he needed.

There were parrots of all shapes and sizes. There was only one problem. They were all too expensive.

As Charlie turned to go, the parrot seller called him back.

"I suppose you could have this one," he said.

Charlie had never seen such a pretty parrot and he was amazed it was so cheap. "You've got a very special bird there!" said the parrot seller.

Now he had his parrot, Charlie wasted no time in setting off on his hunt for treasure.

Out at sea, Charlie spotted a ship named the *Fat Flounder.* He knew it belonged to a rich sailor named Captain Silverside. "I bet that ship is loaded with cash," said Charlie, happily.

Charlie waited until the sailors had gone to lunch. Then he rowed across to the ship and sneaked in through an open window.

Charlie was in luck. He'd climbed into the cabin where the captain kept his treasure.

But he had only just begun to stuff his pockets with gold coins, when disaster struck.

"Sssh!" Charlie hissed at his parrot. But it was too late.

Charlie took one look at Captain
Silverside and ran.

COME BACK HERE,
YOU SNEAKY THIEF!

The captain
and his men
chased Charlie
around the deck
six times before
the poor pirate
escaped to
his boat.

As he rowed back to his ship, Charlie turned to his parrot with a face like thunder. "Don't ever do that again, you pesky parrot!" he scolded.

But every time they went to sea, the parrot caused trouble.

Just as Charlie was about to steal someone's treasure, the parrot let out a warning cry.

Each time, Charlie only just managed
to escape. Soon, he was a nervous wreck.
Whenever he tried
to get rid of
the parrot...

...it always found its way
back to Charlie's shoulder.

As Charlie was eating his supper one evening, he wondered what he could do.

The Laughing Lobster Inn

Super Deluxe Menu

Scrummy Scampi — 7 pennies
Mouthwatering Mussels — 6 pennies

Deluxe Menu

Crispy Cod — 5 pennies
Fancy Fishcakes — 4 pennies

Cheap Menu

Shrimp on toast — 2 pennies

Very Cheap Menu

Bread & cheese — 1 penny

He had never felt so miserable. Thanks to that pesky parrot he was a useless, practically penniless pirate.

Charlie's long face was making the other customers lose their appetites. The landlord tried to cheer him up.

They were so busy talking, neither of them spotted a thief creeping up to the landlord's cash box.

The thief was just about to swipe all the money, when Charlie's parrot squawked into action.

"What a wonderful bird!" said the landlord. "That thief nearly got away with my cash."

This gave Charlie an idea. Perhaps he could put his parrot to good use after all.

The landlord paid Charlie handsomely for his new burglar alarm...

STOP THIEF!

the parrot enjoyed its new job...

...and Charlie had enough money to buy another bird – a quiet one this time.

The Little Mermaid

Far out at sea,
below the waves,
deeper
and deeper
and deeper still,
stood the
Sea King's castle.

There, at the very bottom of the sea, the water was as clear as glass. The sand was as fine as powder. Tall seaweed grew up around the castle walls and small, bright fish darted among its branches.

The Sea King was very proud of his castle. It was the perfect place to bring up his six mermaid daughters.

Each daughter was given her
own small garden to care for.
"I'm going to shape mine like
a whale," said the eldest.

"Mine will have a
seashell border,"
said the next.

"And I'm going to grow
pretty flowers," said the third.

The fourth and fifth mermaids loved exploring. "Let's decorate our gardens with treasure from shipwrecks," they said.

Then their little sister appeared, hugging a statue of a smiling boy. "Look what I've found!" she cried. "I'm going to put him in my garden."

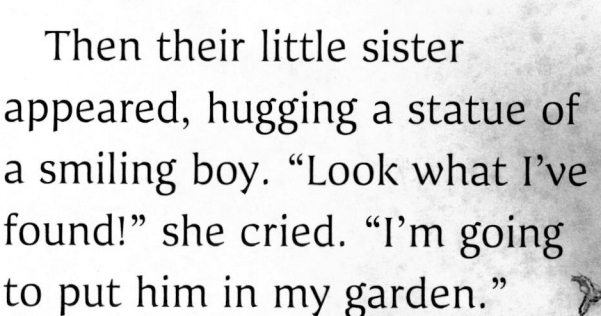

The sisters spent all day in the castle waters,
tending their gardens and playing games.
In the evening, as the sea turned to inky black,
their grandmother called them inside for supper.

Mermaids!

Lying on silky cushions, the family ate
steaming seaweed parcels and soft sea fruits.

298

"Tell us a story, Grandmama,"
begged the littlest mermaid.
   Grandmama had seen the world
above the waves. She told amazing
tales of men with two legs and no tail.

   "There are buildings as tall as the ocean
is deep," she said, "and machines that
glide even faster than sharks."

The little mermaid hung on her every word. "When you reach fifteen," announced the Sea King, "you may rise above the waves and see these things for yourselves."

While the older sisters flicked their tails in delight, the little mermaid sat drumming her fingers. "That's six whole years away!" she sighed.

On the eldest sister's fifteenth
birthday, the Sea King's castle
frothed with excitement.

The mermaids showered their big sister with twinkling pearls. But the best present of all was the Sea King's blessing.

"Now you can swim to the surface of the sea," he said.

"Come back quickly!" called the little mermaid. She wanted to hear everything about the world above.

Her sister finally returned, grinning with excitement. "I watched the sun sink into the sea," she said. "Its orange light flooded the water."

Ooooooooooh!

Ooooooooooooooh!

Ooooooooooh!

Were you afraid?

Did you see land?

Were there any boats?

For hours, the mermaids pestered her with questions. Her littlest sister was the most curious. "Did the wind stroke your hair?" she asked. "Did the sun kiss your cheeks?"

That night, the little mermaid gazed at the sea above. A black blot glided through the water.

"It must be a ship!" she thought. "I wonder who's on it and where they're going...?" She fell asleep and dreamed of sailing the ocean.

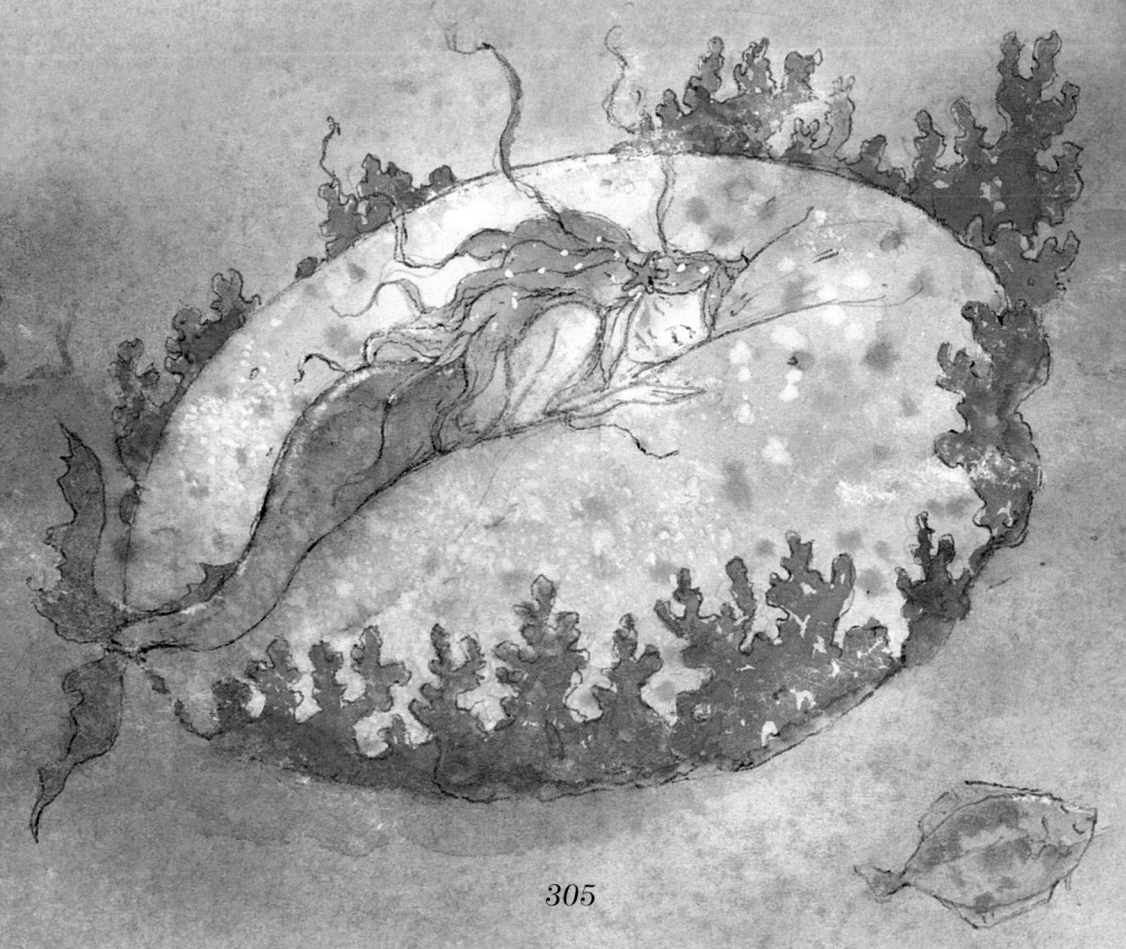

I wonder what air feels like?

One by one, the sisters reached fifteen and were allowed to swim above the waves. The little mermaid watched them rise up, hand in hand, longing for the day she could join them.

As time dragged on, the little mermaid spent hours with her statue. "I can't wait to see what dry land looks like," she told him.

Finally, the year... then the month... then the day of her fifteenth birthday arrived. As soon as the celebrations were over, she set off for the surface.

"Goodbye!" she called to her sisters, rising up like a bubble of air. With each swish of her tail, the water felt lighter.

Her head broke through the waves and she gasped. The sun was setting, just as her sister had described. And there, ahead, floated a ship.

The little mermaid swam closer. Lanterns hung from the masts and lively music filled the air. Closer still, she saw people dancing on deck.

She stared in delight as their two legs carried them back and forth. A handsome young man appeared, wearing a crown.

"Happy birthday, Prince Milo!" the people shouted, as a hundred rockets exploded in the sky.

The little mermaid watched the prince, enchanted. It was as if her statue had come to life.

Suddenly, the weather turned stormy and everyone ran below deck. Waves rose up like mountains around the creaking ship and a streak of lightning split the dark clouds.

The little mermaid rode the surf with glee, but then she heard cries from the ship. The wind and waves were battering it apart, tossing terrified people into the foaming sea.

The mermaid was horrified. "They'll
never survive without tails," she thought.
"Oh, the poor prince. I must find him..."

She searched everywhere,

diving between beams and planks.

At last she saw him,
clinging to a broken mast.

She pulled the prince to a sheltered
cove and let the waves wash him ashore.
"Thank you," he murmured.

The little mermaid watched from a clump
of seaweed. As the dawn light warmed the
sky, a pretty girl came and helped the prince
to his feet. Smiling, he looked out to sea,
then walked away.

The little mermaid
floated joyfully
back to the castle.
"How was it?"
her sisters asked
together.
"Beautiful,"
she sighed.

All day, the sisters played in the castle waters.

"Catch!" cried the eldest, throwing a
sponge ball.

But the little mermaid was too busy dreaming
of walking with her prince.

That night, and every night for a week,
she swam back to the cove and gazed
longingly at the empty beach.

At dawn, she returned to her statue under the sea. "Will I ever see my prince again?" she asked. The marble boy just smiled.

"Why do you swim to the same place each night?" asked her sisters, one morning. The little mermaid blushed and told them about her prince.

"I've seen that prince," said the eldest sister. "He lives in a grand palace by the sea."

"Really?" cried the excited little mermaid. "Show me!"

That evening, all six mermaids rose up through the sea and swam to the palace.

It stood proud and shiny at the water's edge. As the mermaids watched, a man strode onto the balcony.

"It's my prince!" cried the little mermaid. "Do you think he's looking for me?"

"Don't be silly," said the eldest sister.

Day after day, the little mermaid returned to the palace. Each time, she swam a little closer.

When the prince went sailing, she swam behind him. She prayed for a storm, so she could save him again. But it never came.

Back beneath the waves,
the sisters were decorating
the castle for a summer ball.
"Come and help us,"
they called to the
little mermaid.

She tried to tie ribbons, but she just couldn't concentrate.

"You're not still thinking about that prince, are you?" said her eldest sister.

The little mermaid nodded.

"Remember, he's a man and you're a mermaid," her sister went on. "He will only make you unhappy."

By nightfall, the sea castle looked splendid. Blue flames rose up from pearly white shells, lighting the way from the gardens to the hall.

Guests streamed in, wearing shimmery clothes...

...and a fish band sang gurgling tunes.

323

The little mermaid pretended to join in, but she couldn't stop thinking of her prince. "I have to do something," she thought. "Maybe the sea witch can help me..."

While her sisters swayed to the fish band's songs, the little mermaid swam away.

It was a dark and dangerous journey to the sea witch's cave. The little mermaid crossed bubbling hot mud...

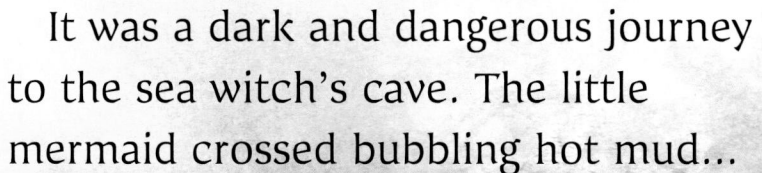

dodged swirling whirlpools...

...and darted past slimy seaweed arms.

At last, the craggy cave loomed up ahead.
The ugly sea witch stood at the entrance.
　"So you want legs to impress a prince,"
she snapped. (The sea witch knew
everything.) "They will cost you dearly."

"But I have nothing to give you,"
said the little mermaid.

"Yes you do," the witch declared. "Your voice."

The little mermaid gulped. "But how will I talk to my prince?" she asked.

"That's not my problem."

The witch started stirring a potion. "This will split your tail in two," she said, "and give you human legs."

"But there are two things you should know," she added. "One, if you drink this potion, you can never go back to your father's castle. And two, if the prince doesn't return your love... you will dissolve into the ocean waves."

The witch stopped stirring and looked up. "Do you still want to drink it?" she asked.

The little mermaid didn't pause. "I do," she replied. They were the last words she ever spoke.

With a wave of her wand, the witch added the mermaid's voice to her potion.

By dawn, the little mermaid was sitting on a sea rock near the palace. In her trembling hand she held a bottle of the witch's potion.

Suddenly, a door opened and the prince stepped onto his balcony. He stretched, yawned and gazed out to sea.

The sight of the prince made the mermaid bolder. She swallowed the potion, jumped into the water... spluttered, splashed and nearly drowned. Her tail had split into legs.

The prince saw the splashes. "Who's that?"
he called. "Somebody help her."

A servant waded in and pulled the little
mermaid to safety. Soon she was standing
in front of her prince.

"Who are you?" he asked.

She couldn't answer. He asked again.

She still couldn't answer. Instead, she smiled.

The prince smiled back. "Find this young lady some clothes," he said to his servant. "She's joining me for breakfast."

The little mermaid spent the whole day with the prince. She was very happy but kept wobbling on her new feet.

"Take my arm," said the prince. "I'll show you around."

That evening, the little mermaid stood on the prince's balcony. Frothy waves danced on the rocks below. Five tails flipped by and she recognized her sisters.

"Come back!" they cried.

The little mermaid smiled but shook her head. She had made her choice.

"I don't even know your name," the prince was saying. "But when I saw you in the water this morning, I thought of my own true love."

The mermaid's eyes sparkled and her heart beat faster.

"I almost drowned once," he went on. "I was swept to a beach and woken by a lovely princess. Tomorrow I'm going to set sail and marry her!"

The prince's words were like a dagger in the mermaid's heart. He was everything to her, but he loved someone else.

"Don't worry," he said. "You can come with me."

But the little mermaid shook her head, sobbing silently.

Next morning, she watched her prince sail into the distance.

The world she loved was lost to her. "You can never go back," said the witch's voice inside her head.

"Come to us," sang the ocean spray.

"Forever," whispered the foaming surf. With tears streaming down her cheeks, the brave little mermaid disappeared into the welcoming waves.

Fairy in a flap

Poppy was almost a perfect fairy.

Her wand twinkled,
her wings shone and her
spells never went wrong.

But Poppy had a problem...

...she couldn't fly.

At school, her friends soared into the sky. Poppy couldn't get off the ground.

"Just keep trying," said the teacher. Poppy flapped her wings until they hurt, but she didn't even hover.

Her mother took her to the fairy doctor.
"Hmm..." he said. "Stretch out like a butterfly."
Poppy's wings fluttered open.

"She seems fine," he said, "but try
this potion." He mixed a little honey
with some fluffy clouds.

The potion was delicious, but it didn't help Poppy fly.

"How do you do it?" she asked her best friend, Daisy.

Daisy shrugged. "It just happens," she said.

"You're so lucky," said Poppy, sadly.

"Well, you're better at spells than me," said Daisy.

While her friends did aerobatics,
Poppy was stuck in the baby class.
As she flapped her wings, a tear
rolled down her cheek.

Just then, an imp went past.
"What a big baby," he jeered.

Poppy ran from the class sobbing.
She didn't stop until she reached the forest.
Still crying, she hid in a hollow tree.

"Whooo's that?" hooted an owl grumpily.
"Why the fuss?"

345

Hiccuping, Poppy told him.

"Imps are so rude," tutted the owl.
"As for learning to fly, I can teach you.
I've taught hundreds of fledglings."

"Jump off a low branch," he ordered, "and flap your wings."

Concentrating hard, Poppy jumped, flapped... and dropped straight to the ground.

"Oooh dear," the owl hooted. "You're thinking about it too much. Never mind. We'll try again tomorrow."

Back at home, Poppy was making a bandage from blackberry leaves when Daisy burst in. "I've found a spell to make you fly!" she squealed excitedly.

Before Poppy could stop her, Daisy had waved her wand and gabbled a spell.

Leave the ground and touch the sky...
Voll-ah-ray Poppy...
...you will fly!

"I feel the same," Poppy said, doubtfully. "Try it!" urged Daisy, pushing her through the door. "I won't watch."

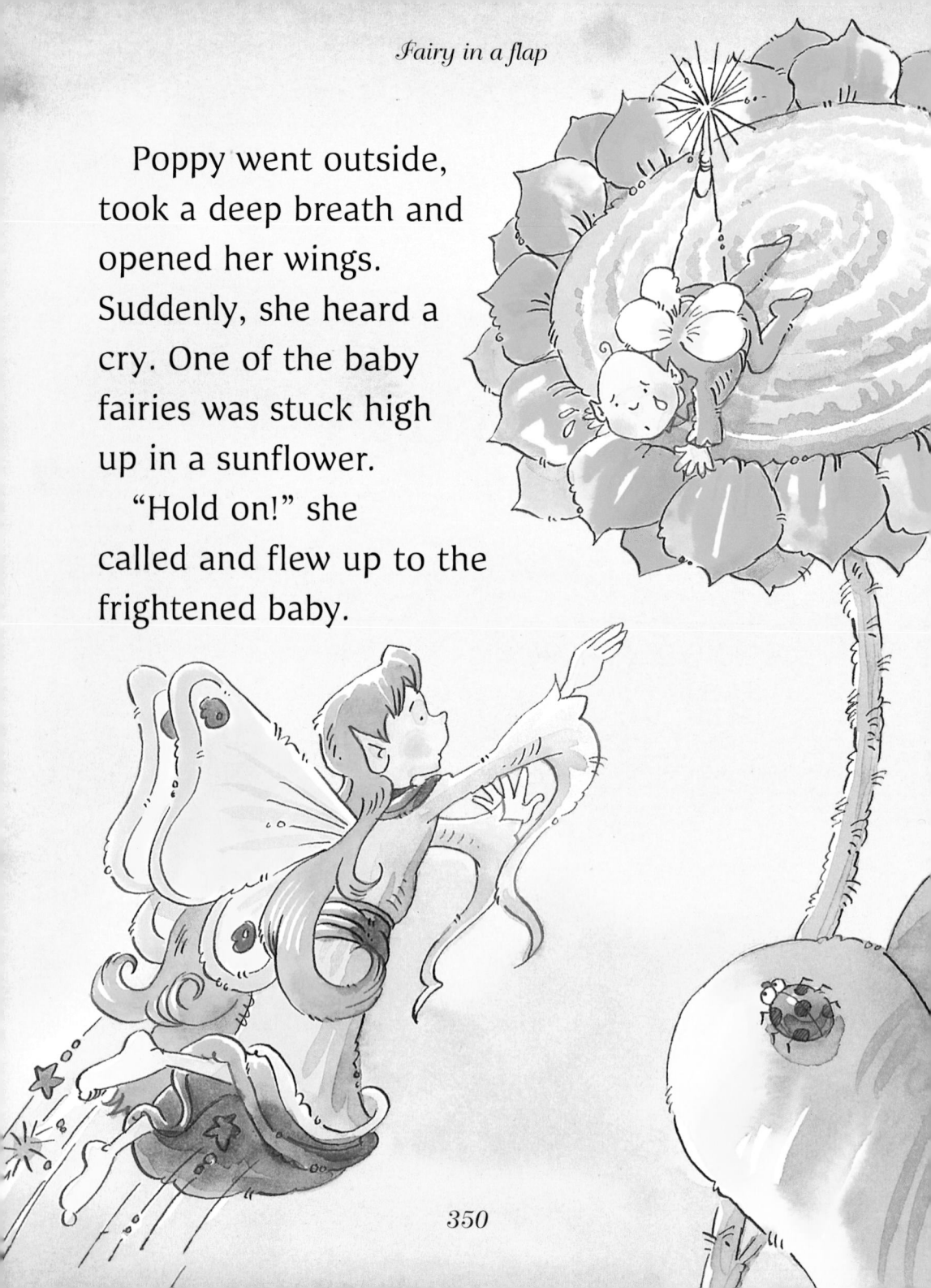

Poppy went outside, took a deep breath and opened her wings. Suddenly, she heard a cry. One of the baby fairies was stuck high up in a sunflower.

"Hold on!" she called and flew up to the frightened baby.

As she fluttered back down, Daisy raced out.
"Poppy, wait. I got the spell wrong..."
She stopped. "Poppy?"

"Yes," said Poppy, with
a big grin. "I can fly!"

Treasure Island

This is the story of my incredible adventure on Treasure Island. I'm Jim Hawkins and I help my mother run the Admiral Benbow Inn...

Each day was just like the last, until the morning a stranger arrived.

I was sweeping, when an old sea captain strode up the road, singing. He saw me and stopped outside the inn.

"Many people here?" he growled. I shook my head. "Then I'll stay," said the captain.

Can you
do something
for me?

"Name's Billy Bones," he told me, giving me a silver coin. "Look out for a sailor with one leg," he whispered, "and I'll give you a coin every month."

During the day, Billy Bones strode along the cliffs peering at the sea through his telescope. At night, he told scary stories about pirates. He stayed for months, but he never paid my mother a penny.

And old Captain Scar stood alone on the deck with his jagged cutlass in his hand...

One frosty morning, when Billy Bones was out, a man came to the inn.

"Is there a captain staying here?" he asked. Just then, Bones strode through the door. "Hello Bill," said the man. Bones looked as though he had seen a ghost.

"Black Dog!" gasped Bones.
"Yes," sneered the man,
"and I've come for what's
hidden in that sea chest
of yours."

You'll never get
your hands on it,
you interfering devil!

With a clang of steel, both men drew
their swords. Bones struck Black Dog on the
shoulder and chased him out of the inn.

Bones was so shocked that he grew sick and had to stay in bed. "You've got to help me Jim," he begged. "Black Dog sailed with a pirate named Captain Flint. Now his whole crew will be after me. If you ever see strange men hanging around, get help!"

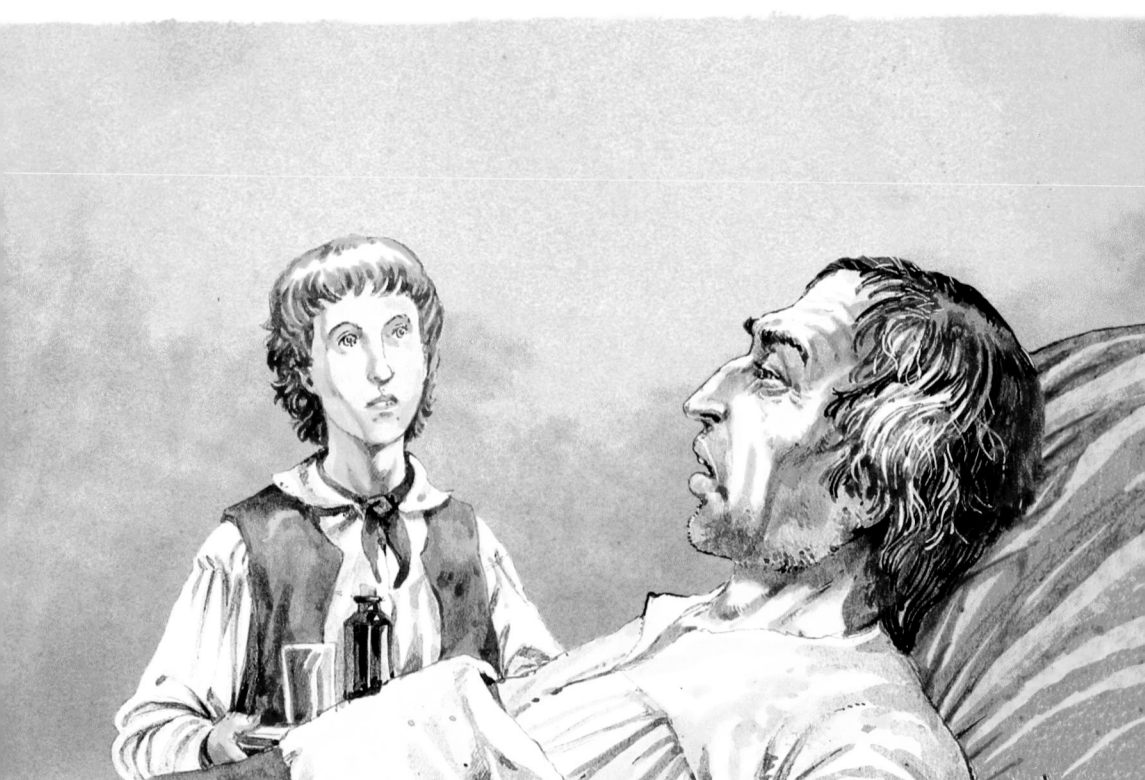

Only a few days later, I heard an odd noise outside. Tap... tap... tap... A blind man was trudging along, tapping the road with his stick.

"Where am I?" he asked.

"The Admiral Benbow Inn," I replied.

The man grabbed my arm with an icy hand. "Take me to Billy Bones," he hissed.

When Bones saw the blind man, he was horrified. The man gave Bones a note and hurried away.

With trembling fingers, Bones read the message. "The pirates!" he gasped. "They're coming tonight!" With a cry of pain, he fell to the floor. To my horror, he was dead.

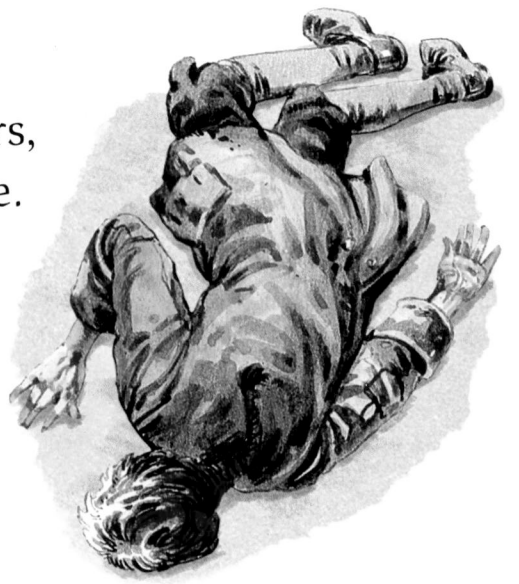

I didn't like the sound of those pirates at all. But Mother was determined to see what Bones had hidden in his chest. So, that night, I locked all the doors and windows of the inn and we went to the captain's room.

His chest was full of old clothes and weapons, but at the very bottom we found papers and a bag of gold.

Excitedly, we began to count the money. Just then, someone rattled the door of the inn. Then I heard a faint tapping. Tap... tap... tap...

We grabbed the money and papers and ran out into the night. I'd only just pulled my mother into a hiding place when a gang of men rushed to the inn.

They smashed down the door and stormed through our home, shouting, "Bones is dead! Find the papers!"

Suddenly the blind man threw open a window.

"The papers have gone!" he shrieked. "Find the boy!"

But as the pirates came closer to our hiding place, a group of soldiers galloped over the hill.

The pirates fled.

"We heard you were in danger," the captain of the soldiers said to me. "Sorry we took so long."

"The pirates wanted these papers," I explained. "I think we should take them to the Hall and show Squire Trelawny."

Where did you get them?

We found them in Billy Bones' chest.

Squire Trelawny was having dinner with his friend Dr. Livesey. They were amazed by my story.

When Dr. Livesey opened the packet of papers, he found a map.

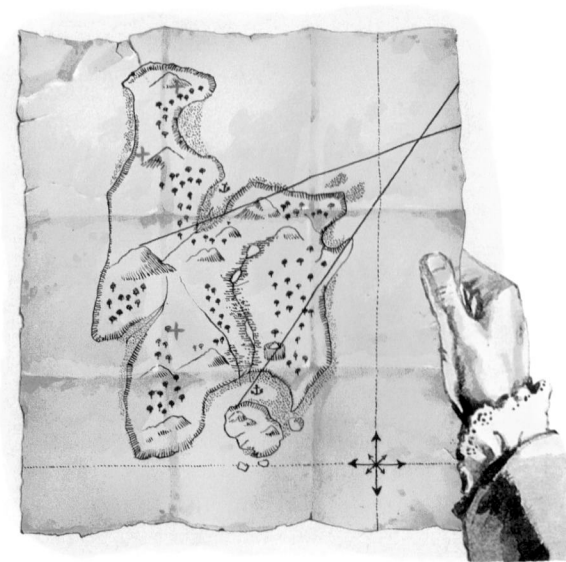

"No wonder Flint's pirates wanted this," he said. "It shows where his treasure is buried!"

Squire Trelawny was thrilled. "Here's my plan," he said. "We shall sail to that island and find Flint's treasure. And you, Jim, can come with us!"

But don't tell anyone about the treasure!

So, a month later, I hugged my mother goodbye and set off to Bristol docks. The Squire looked very excited. "There's our ship," he said. "She's called the *Hispaniola*."

He asked me to take a message to the ship's cook, Long John Silver. I was horrified to see he had only one leg. Was this the sailor Bones had paid me to watch out for? He seemed friendly enough.

Thank'ee kindly, Jim lad.

Besides, I had something else to worry about.

Captain Smollett, who was in charge of the *Hispaniola*, was angry. "I thought this voyage was a secret," he snapped, "but it seems the whole crew knows you're after Flint's treasure. I don't trust them."

Those sailors are a shifty-looking bunch, if you ask me!

We were all worried by the captain's news, but it was too late to find a new crew. The next morning, we set sail.

Pieces of eight! Lovely boy!

During the voyage, I made friends with Long John. I liked the talking parrot who sat on his shoulder.

But one night, I was climbing into a barrel to get an apple...

Almost got it!

Sounds good! What's the plan?

...when I overheard Long John whispering to a young sailor. "I was Captain Flint's second-in-command," he said. "Join us pirates and get rich."

I broke out in a sweat. Captain Smollett was right. Some of the men were pirates.

"We'll wait until we have the treasure," continued Long John, "then we'll kill the captain and his friends."

"Oh no!" I thought. "I've got to tell the others."

Just then there was a cry of "Land ahoy!"
Everyone rushed onto the deck to look at
Treasure Island.

I ran to the captain's cabin and told
everyone what I'd heard.

"We can't give up now!" said the captain.
"We must find out
who's on our
side and be
ready to fight."

Next morning, we arrived at the island. The men wanted to lie on the beach. Instead, they had to mend sails and scrub the decks. The sailors started grumbling.

Captain Smollett, scared they'd rebel, gave them the afternoon off.

The sailors eagerly rowed for the shore. I was desperate to go too, so I slipped into one of the boats.

When we reached the beach, I jumped out and ran off into the trees. I couldn't wait to have a look around the island.

I was exploring the island when I heard Long John Silver talking to one of the sailors.

Join us pirates or you'll pay the price!

The sailor turned and ran. With a growl, Long John hurled his walking stick, knocking the man down and killing him.

He KILLED him!

I ran away into the forest, stumbling and gasping.

But then I saw a shadowy figure dodge behind a tree. As I drew closer, a wild man sprang out!

Don't hurt me! I'm only poor Ben Gunn.

"My pirate friends left me here to die," said Ben. "Please help me escape from the island. I'll make you rich if you do."

Just at that moment, the distant boom of a cannon shook the air. "I must go and help my friends!" I thought.

Meanwhile, as I found out later, Dr. Livesey was searching for me with one of the sailors. They came across a fort made of logs on a hill.

Suddenly, they heard a piercing scream from the ship. "The pirates are attacking," said the doctor. "Quick! We'll get the others and hide here."

The pair rushed back to the ship, helped the captain load a boat with guns and rowed desperately for the shore. Some pirates fired at them with the ship's cannon, but they reached the land safely.

So, as I ran across the island, I saw the captain's flag fluttering over the log fort. I scrambled over the fence and dashed inside.

"I've just seen Long John Silver kill a sailor!" I cried, panting. "And, when I ran away, I met a man called Ben Gunn in the woods!"

"Silver killed a sailor?" said the Squire, looking worried.

"We don't have many guns," added Dr. Livesey, "and the pirates are fierce fighters."

We stayed up all night, trying to decide what to do. But, as the sun came up, we still didn't have a plan.

At dawn, Long John Silver came hobbling up the hill. "Give us the treasure map," he said, "and we won't harm you."

"We don't bargain with pirates," said the captain.

"Then you're all dead men," sneered Long John and walked off.

The captain looked at us.

"Get ready to fight, my lads," he said. Time seemed to stop. It became very hot and quiet.

Suddenly, shots rang out and pirates swarmed over the fence. The captain's men opened fire and a savage battle began.

Finally, the fighting was over and the last few pirates ran off, defeated. Dr. Livesey took the treasure map and disappeared into the woods.

I guessed he had gone to find Ben Gunn and I wanted to help. Taking two pistols, I crept away to join him.

But, as I walked along the beach,
I found a boat Ben Gunn had made. It
gave me a wonderful idea. I would cut the
Hispaniola loose from its rope. With luck,
the few pirates left on board would be taken
by surprise and the ship would run aground!
"I'll give those pirates something to think
about," I thought.

It was easy to launch the little boat into the waves, but it wasn't so easy to steer it. When I tried to paddle, the boat just spun in circles.

Luckily, the tide swept me over to the ship. Catching hold of the anchor rope, I sliced through it.

I could hear people shouting inside, so I quietly crawled up to a window. Two pirates were locked in a vicious fight.

The ship moved suddenly, startling the pirates. I dived back into my boat and crouched at the bottom. I hid, with my eyes shut, as the waves carried me out to sea.

Hours later, I woke with my head spinning. It was already daytime and I was bobbing on the sea not far from the island. But, when I tried to paddle ashore, the boat was caught by a huge wave and plunged underwater for a second.

I was terrified. I realized I had no control over the boat and feared I'd be lost at sea forever. Then, to my great relief, I saw the *Hispaniola* drifting my way. There was only one thing to do. I would have to get on board and try to take charge.

All of a sudden, the ship reared up on the sea and towered over me. I sprang up and managed to catch hold of it, just as it smashed the little boat to tiny pieces.

Holding on with all my strength, I clambered along a mast as the ship rocked and plunged.

Gently, I swung myself down onto the deck. The whole place seemed strangely quiet.

In a corner, two pirates were lying in a pool of blood. One was dead, but the other groaned and looked up. It was Israel Hands, one of Long John Silver's friends.

What are you doing here?

I've come to take the ship back to Captain Smollett!

Hands smiled slyly. "I'll help you sail the ship to the island if you like," he offered.

But as we approached a bay, I heard a noise behind me. I whirled around. Hands was clutching a dagger, ready to strike.

What are
you doing?

Getting the ship
back!

He lunged at me, but I skipped to one side. Then I tried to fire one of the pistols... There was only a dull click.

In desperation, I scrambled up the mast ropes, climbing higher and higher.

You can't escape that easily, lad!

At one point
I glanced down.
Hands was climbing
after me! I paused
to reload my
pistols.

Suddenly, Hands
hurled his dagger,
striking me on the
shoulder. I have
never felt such pain,
before or since.

As I shouted out,
both pistols went
off. Hands screamed
and dropped into
the sea.

Aaargh!

With a thumping heart and throbbing shoulder, I climbed down and swam ashore. I'd escaped. And now the *Hispaniola* was ready for the captain. Eagerly, I set off across the island to find my friends.

When I finally reached the log fort, it was dark. I crept inside, stumbling in the gloom.

Suddenly, a weird voice shrieked, "Pieces of eight!" It was the parrot. I tried to run, but someone grabbed me and held up a light.

To my dismay, I was surrounded by pirates!
"Your friends have gone," Long John said.
"There's only us now." Another pirate snarled
and lunged at me with a knife. "Hey!" growled
Long John, "I'm in charge here."

The pirates glared at him. "We want a new leader," one of them said. Long John took something out of his pocket and held it up.

Everyone gasped: Flint's treasure map! I was puzzled, but Long John wouldn't tell me how it came into his hands.

THREE CHEERS FOR OLD SILVER!

Next morning, to my surprise, Dr. Livesey arrived. He'd agreed to look after the wounded pirates.

Long John was determined to keep me a prisoner, but he let me talk to the doctor for a while.

"I thought you'd gone," I said, telling Dr. Livesey about my adventure on the *Hispaniola*.

Well done, Jim! Don't worry, we'll rescue you.

Soon after breakfast, the pirates set off to find the treasure. They took me with them.

"However will I escape?" I thought in a panic.

The map said Flint's chest was buried under a tall tree in the shadow of Spyglass Hill.

As we neared the spot marked "X" on the map, a pirate up ahead began to shout. But he hadn't found treasure... He'd found a skeleton.

In the silence that followed, a spine-chilling voice filled the air. It sang a sailor's song. "The ghost of Captain Flint!" cried the pirates.

Flint is coming to get us! RUN!

"Don't be stupid," said Long John. "It's just someone trying to scare us."

Another pirate spotted a tall tree and everyone charged over to it. But at the bottom of the tree was an empty hole. The treasure had gone.

Long John has dragged us all this way for nothing!

Long John tapped me on my good shoulder. "There's going to be trouble," he whispered. Was he on our side now?

I clutched my pistols tightly, feeling sweat run down my neck.

The men are going to be furious. Get ready to fight!

The pirates stared at Long John menacingly and drew their guns. Just then, shots rang out. Dr. Livesey and Ben Gunn charged out of the bushes with a sailor named Gray. The terrified pirates ran off.

"Quick!" said the doctor. "We must get to the boats before the pirates." We sprinted to the beach, with Long John hobbling behind.

"Don't leave me!" he panted. "The others will kill me."

I'll damage this boat, so the pirates can't follow us!

We clambered aboard a boat and rowed for the *Hispaniola*.

As Gray rowed, Dr. Livesey cleared up a mystery. "I tricked Silver with the treasure map," he told me. "I wanted to distract the pirates. I knew Ben had found Flint's treasure years ago."

Leaving Gray behind to guard the *Hispaniola*, the rest of us headed for Ben's cave and the treasure.

The Squire and Captain Smollett are waiting for us in Ben's cave.

Ben's cave was enormous. The ground was covered in huge heaps of glittering coins, gold bars and jewels that gleamed in the firelight.

The Squire and Captain Smollett were thrilled to see me. That night, we had a grand feast to celebrate finding Flint's treasure.

Next morning, we loaded up the ship with the treasure and sailed away. We took Long John along, but during the voyage, Ben Gunn helped him escape with some gold.

"I thought we'd be better off without him," Ben said.

When we landed at Bristol docks, I hugged everyone goodbye and took my share of the gold. I never saw Long John Silver again.

I never did go back to Treasure Island, but sometimes, in my dreams, I hear the waves on the sand or Long John's parrot squawking, "Pieces of Eight!"

The tale
of the
kitchen
knight

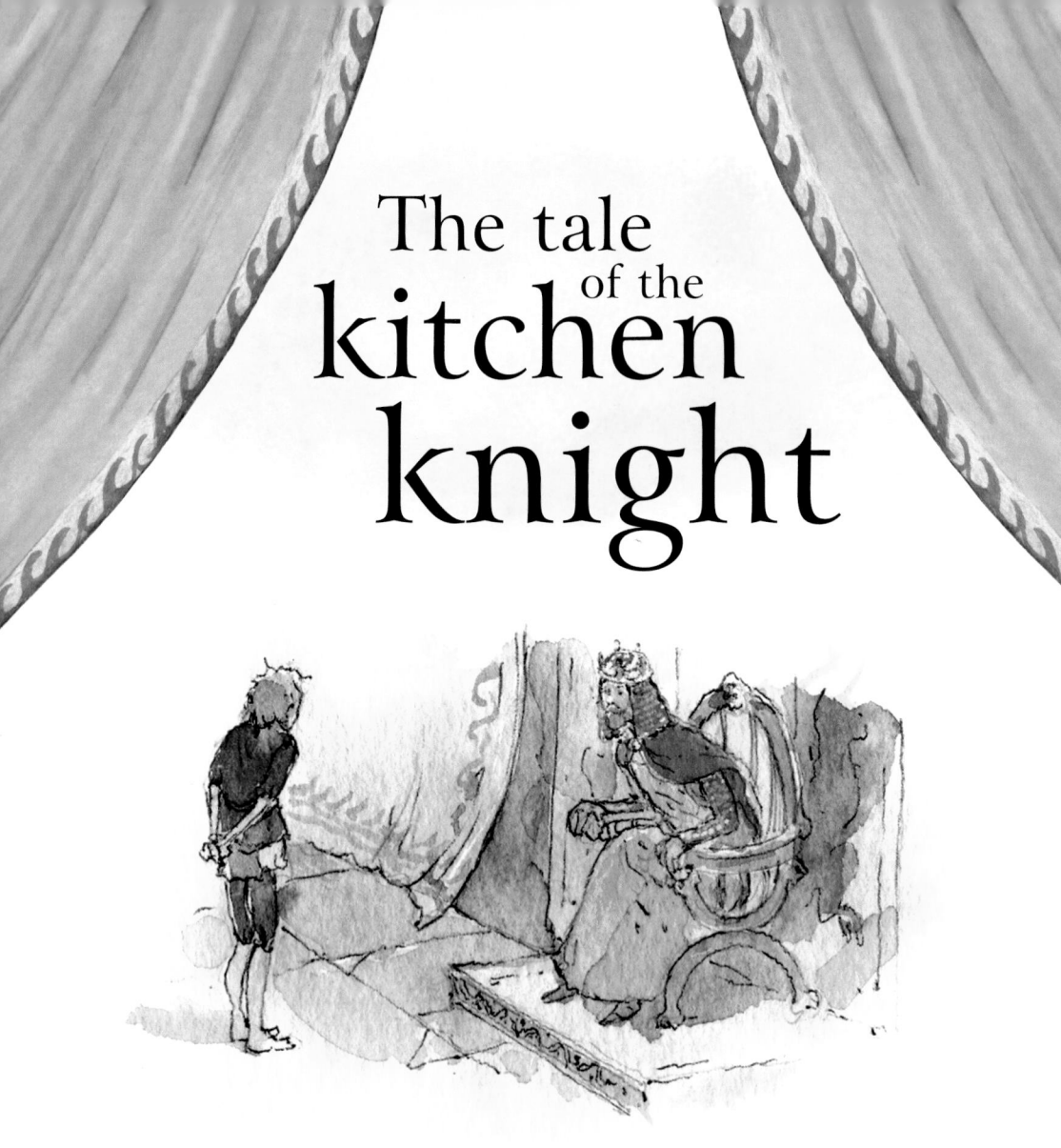

One day, a young stranger arrived at King Arthur's castle. He had beautiful white hands but his clothes were old and torn.

"I have nowhere to go," he told the king.
"Please Sire, may I stay for a year?"

King Arthur liked the look of him, so he
agreed. "Sir Kay can take care of you," he said.

Grumpy Sir Kay was in charge of the kitchens. He sneered at the young boy. "Hmph! I shall call you Pretty Hands," he said. "Now, let's see how hard you can work."

Work harder, Pretty Hands!

Pretty Hands stirred soup...

peeled vegetables...

mopped floors...

and washed dishes.

He even chopped
wood. But he
never complained.

When Pretty Hands had been at the castle for almost a year, a lady came to Camelot. Her name was Linnet and she was very rude.

"Get me a knight! I need help!" she declared. "My sister Lyonesse has been captured by the Red Knight."

The Red Knight!

He's as strong as seven men!

No one wanted to help Linnet. Then Pretty Hands stepped forward. "I'll rescue your sister," he announced.

Everyone was shocked. He was only the kitchen boy.

Lady Linnet was furious. "I want a real knight," she stormed, "not a boy who smells of the kitchen!"

"Don't worry, my Lady," said King Arthur. "Sir Lancelot will make him into a real knight first."

Just before he was knighted, Pretty Hands told Sir Lancelot a secret. His real name was Gareth and he was Sir Gawain's brother.

Arise, Sir Gareth!

The next day, Sir Gareth set off with Lady Linnet to rescue her sister. They faced dragons and worse. Gareth killed them all, but Linnet wasn't impressed.

At last, they reached the Red
Knight's castle. Lady Lyonesse
was locked in a tower. When
she saw Sir Gareth she smiled.
Gareth took one look at her and
fell in love.

Fair lady, I promise
I will set you free!

Gareth rode up to the castle and hammered on the door. There was a terrible roar. Then the door opened and the Red Knight thundered out.

I'll tear you to pieces!

Just you try!

Sir Gareth and the Red Knight fought for hours. It was a hard battle and both of them were badly wounded. But, as the sun sank and the stars rose, Sir Gareth finally won.

Mercy!

Leaving the Red Knight on the ground, Gareth raced to the tower and unlocked Lady Lyonesse. Before she could say a word, he asked her to marry him.

Oh, yes!

Will you be my wife?

Back at Camelot, King Arthur gave the couple a grand wedding. When Gareth told him his real name, he was welcomed to the Round Table to sit beside his brother.

"Not bad – for a kitchen boy!" said Lady Linnet.

Sir Gawain and the Green Knight

It was New Year's Eve in the kingdom of Camelot and King Arthur was holding a feast.

Everyone was sitting around the table, eating, laughing and talking. There was music playing and there'd be dancing later.

In fact everyone was having more fun than they'd had in along time when...

...a giant knight strode into the hall. He was as big as a bear and looked as wild as a wolf. But the strangest thing about him was – he was completely green.

The giant looked at King Arthur's knights, seated around the table. After a pause, he roared, "Which of you will play a New Year's game with me? You chop off my head, then I'll chop off yours!"

No one wanted to play his game. But the Green Knight refused to leave. Finally, Sir Gawain agreed. Seizing the giant's massive sword, he sliced off his green head.

Everyone gasped as the head bounced down the hall like a huge green ball.

Then the Green Knight's body calmly bent down, picked up the head and tucked it under his arm.

The head looked up. "Well done, Sir Gawain!" it said. "Now it's my turn."

Sir Gawain turned pale.

"You have a year and a day," the head went on. "Meet me at the Green Chapel next New Year's Day."

But where's the Green Chapel?

You must find it yourself.

The following winter, Sir Gawain set off. He knew he was riding to certain death but he had given his word.

Can you tell me where to find the Green Chapel?

I've never heard of it.

He searched the kingdom with no success. By Christmas he was exhausted, but he would not give up.

At last, Sir Gawain came to a castle in a forest, owned by the lord Sir Bertilak. Sir Gawain asked his question and Sir Bertilak smiled.

"The Green Chapel?" he said. "It's just around the corner."

"Finally!" sighed Gawain.

When Sir Bertilak heard Sir Gawain's story, he asked the knight to stay with him. For three days, Sir Bertilak went out hunting. Gawain stayed at home with Bertilak's wife.

In the evenings, they ate dinner together. The knights told each other everything they had done during the day.

"I chased a stag!" said Bertilak, on the first night.

Gawain blushed. "I read to your wife and she gave me a kiss," he said.

"I chased a boar!" said Bertilak on the second night.

"Your wife kissed me twice," said Gawain, bright red.

"I chased a fox!" said Bertilak on the third night.

"Your wife gave me three kisses," Gawain whispered.

But Gawain kept a secret. Sir Bertilak's wife had also given him a magic belt. She said it could save his life.

Gawain knew he should tell Bertilak. But he wanted to wear it when he met the Green Knight.

On New Year's Day, Sir Gawain rode to the Green Chapel.

The Green Knight was waiting. Telling Gawain to kneel down, he raised his massive sword...

But then he lowered his sword again.

The Green Knight raised his sword for a second time. Again, he put it down.

The third time he raised his sword, Sir Gawain didn't worry. But this time, the Green Knight gave Gawain a painful nick on the neck.

"Why did you do that?" asked Gawain.

The next minute, the giant started
to shrink...

and shrink...

until he
turned into...

Sir Bertilak!

"Yes!" cried Sir Bertilak. "I was the Green Knight. It was a test. I know you're brave because you came to seek me. But I wanted to see how honest a knight you were, too."

"So, I asked my wife to kiss you and give you the belt," Sir Bertilak went on. "Twice, you told me the truth and I didn't harm you. But the third time you kept a secret."

Sir Gawain fell to his knees. "I'm a bad knight," he said. "I'm a coward. You should cut off my head."

"Nonsense!" said Sir Bertilak. "You didn't do that badly. Now, come back to the castle. I've organized a feast."

Gawain smiled, feeling incredibly relieved.

"Oh, and no more games, I promise!" Sir Bertilak chuckled.

The band of robbers

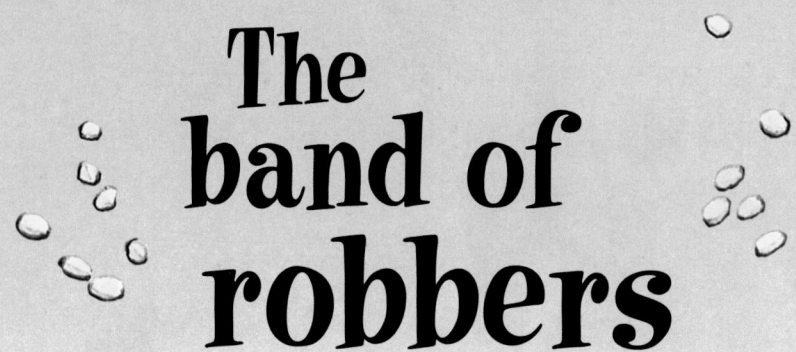

Pinchbeck the wizard and Pogo the goblin were walking together in the woods.

They were talking about a magic spell.

"The mushrooms must be picked at midnight," Pogo told Pinchbeck.

They were so busy talking, they didn't see a robber creeping up behind them.

I spy a bag of gold!

Suddenly, the robber jumped out. He hit
Pinchbeck over the head with his club.
"Give me your gold!" he shouted.

Pinchbeck dropped the gold. Pogo just ran.

The robber tied Pinchbeck to a tree.
Three hours later, Pogo came back.
"My head hurts," groaned Pinchbeck.
"Let's go to the castle for help," said Pogo.

Slowly, Pinchbeck and Pogo climbed to the castle. They stopped in front of a huge wooden door and knocked.

Inside, the king and queen were having tea.

"Was that a knock?" asked the queen, pausing between mouthfuls of soft-boiled egg.

"Hmm, I wonder who it could be?" said the king.

"Who's there?" called the king.

"Pogo!" said Pogo. "With Pinchbeck the wizard."

"We were robbed in the woods. Please let us in."

"That's terrible!" said the king. "Come in at once."

The queen made some fresh tea, and wrapped Pinchbeck's head in bandages.

"The robbers came here too," she said.

"And they're coming back tomorrow," the king added. "If we don't give them two more bags of gold, they'll take over our castle. And we don't have any gold left!"

That night, Pinchbeck and Pogo stayed in the castle. They wished that they could do something to help.

"My head's thumping too much," sighed Pinchbeck. "I can't think of any spells."

But Pogo had an idea. Early the next morning, he sneaked out of the castle. "I hope I don't wake anyone up," he thought.

He found two sacks in a shed and tiptoed through the garden.

If he tried hard enough, he might be able to work a spell. As fast as he could, he stuffed both sacks with leaves.

Then he hurried back to the castle.

When Pinchbeck saw the sacks, he clapped his hands with glee. "Pogo! You've helped me to remember a spell!"

Umpi-grumpi, do as as you're told.
Fool those robbers and turn into gold!

Yellow smoke filled the air, then...

Rat-a-tat-tat! The robbers were banging on the door.

"Open up!" they yelled. "We know you don't have any gold. The castle's ours!"

The queen began to cry. "But we have nowhere to go," she sobbed.

"Tough!" said the robbers.

"Please don't take the castle," pleaded the king.

It's our home!

Just then, the robbers heard another voice. It was Pinchbeck. "Take a look at this," he called, waving at the robbers.

They couldn't believe their eyes. The robbers blinked, and stared, then blinked again.

"Take your gold," said Pinchbeck. "And make sure we never see you here again."

"Ha! We're rich now," said the chief robber. "Why would we come back?"

And they set off. They rode for five days and five nights. The sacks were getting lighter but the robbers didn't notice. At last, they stopped to rest.

Tired and hungry, they decided to cheer themselves up. "Let's count our gold," they said. But all they found in the sacks were....

Leaves?

"It's a trick!" shouted the chief robber, "We'll go back!"

But it was no good. They'd come too far and were completely lost.

At the castle, Pinchbeck's head healed and his spells returned. It was time to go.

But before he left, he gave the king and queen a magic sack of gold which would never run out.

Then he and Pogo headed back into the woods, the way they had come.

The tooth fairy

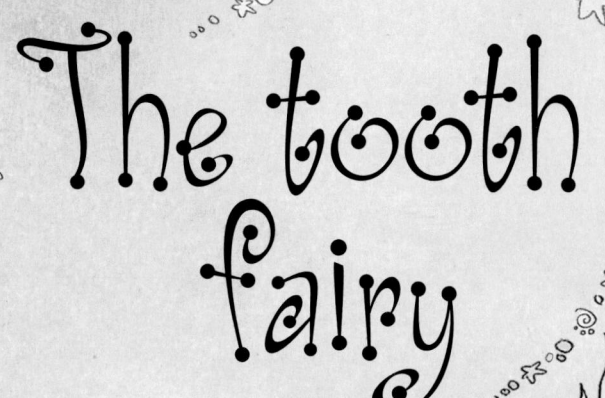

It was a fantastic day for Crystal.
She had passed her final test at
the tooth fairy training school.

Now she could turn children's baby teeth into money.

Jet, Crystal's lazy classmate, had failed all her tests. She would never be a tooth fairy. "It's not fair!" she moaned.

As Jet grumbled, the others flew home and prepared for their first trips.

That night, Crystal checked that she had everything she needed...

one bag of magic travel dust...

Check!

Check!

one list of children to visit...

and, most importantly, her wand.

Check!

Crystal sprinkled herself with magic dust. The next second, she was in the bedroom of her first customer, Beth Bingly.

Crystal flew up to the bed. Carefully, she lifted a tooth out from under Beth's pillow.

She aimed her wand at Beth's tooth.
"*Zapanasha!*" she cried. But instead of
a shiny, new coin, she saw...

A ham sandwich?

A hamster?

A CACTUS?

Every time she aimed her wand, the tooth
changed into something – but never a coin.

Crystal burst into tears. "It's all gone wrong," she sobbed.

Her crying woke Beth, who couldn't believe her eyes.

"Are you the tooth fairy?" she whispered in amazement.

"Yes," wept Crystal, "but it's my first night and I'm useless."

Crystal explained how her wand had failed. "Everyone in Fairyland will laugh at me," she sobbed. "What can I do?"

Beth felt sorry for the fairy. "Let me go back with you," she said. "Maybe I can help."

"Thank you," Crystal sniffed.

A sprinkle of travel dust later, Beth was
in Fairyland. The magic powder had made
her fairy-sized. She could fly, too!

"My wand came from the Fantastic
Fairy Store," explained Crystal.

"Then we'll start there,"
said Beth.

Beth gasped as she entered the shop. The walls were lined with hundreds of fairy outfits.

There were sparkly tiaras, silky bows, shiny shoes and pots and pots of gleaming wands.

"How can I help you?" asked the shopkeeper.

Crystal explained and the shopkeeper examined the wand.

"This is Jet's wand," she said. "It will never work properly, because she's such a bad fairy."

"That sneaky fairy has swapped her wand for mine," cried Crystal.

"Let's get it back," said Beth.

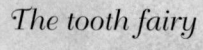

Jet was lazing on the terrace of her tree house. She'd used Crystal's wand to magic up a huge pile of cream cakes.

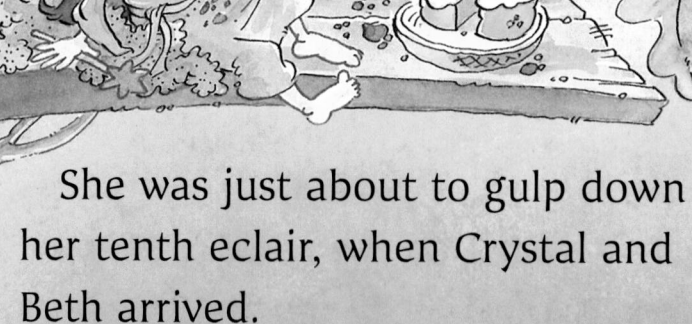

She was just about to gulp down her tenth eclair, when Crystal and Beth arrived.

"Hand over my wand, you thief!" demanded Crystal.

"No way, Miss Perfect," said Jet. A stream
of stars shot from the wand in her hand.
The magical blast turned Crystal's
feet to stone.

Jet raised the wand to strike again. But
suddenly it was snatched from her grasp.
"I'll take that," cried Beth, from a branch
above Jet's head.

Jet tried to fly up and grab the wand back. But she'd eaten so much, she couldn't get off the ground.

A second blast from the wand lifted the stony spell from Crystal's feet. She fluttered up to join Beth. "So long, Jet!" cried Crystal as they flew away.

The pair returned to the Fantastic Fairy Store. Crystal bought Beth her very own fairy outfit to thank her.

Then Beth joined the fairies for a midnight feast and they danced until dawn.

"Time to say goodbye," said Crystal, showering Beth in magic dust.

In a flash, Beth was back in bed. "What an amazing dream," she thought.

Beth peeked under her pillow.
She expected to see her tooth,
or even a coin.

But what she saw was the
tiniest dress in the world.

Robot racers

BOTSVILLE
ROAD RACE

TOMORROW

1st prize - a deluxe
robo-makeover

Squeaky the cleaning robot hated his job. He
was out in all weather, sweeping streets.
What he really wanted was to win the Botsville
road race.

The winning robot would get a new memory chip and a head-to-wheel polish.

But Squeaky didn't dare enter. He was so rusty and clanky, he wasn't sure he could even finish the race.

He was feeling sorry for himself when a noisy robot zoomed past.

Out of the way, rust bucket!

Tanktop was the biggest, meanest robot in town. Everyone was certain he would win tomorrow's big race.

But he wasn't taking any chances. He had a plan to make sure none of the other racers even started.

That night, as the Botsville robots recharged themselves, Tanktop visited each of his rivals in secret.

He gave
Tina Turbo a
puncture...

stole Cyber Sid's
memory chip...

undid Andi Droid's
battery pack...

She'll sleep right
through the race!

and reset Betty Byte's
built-in alarm clock.

The next morning, Tanktop was the only robot at the starting line. It looked as if his plan had worked. The judge was puzzled. "Where is everyone?" he wondered.

"I'll take my prize now," smirked Tanktop. "There must be someone else willing to race," cried the judge desperately. Tanktop was making him look stupid.

Just then a tinny voice piped up. "I will!"
Everyone in the crowd turned. "Is that
Squeaky?" said someone in amazement.

"I'd like to try," said Squeaky. His joints were
feeling especially stiff today, but he couldn't
miss his chance.

"Very well," said the judge, with a sigh of
relief. "Robots, on your marks!"

Tanktop hadn't bothered to charge up his battery that morning. But he was confident he could still beat Squeaky.

The robots set off on their lap of the town. Tanktop raced off with a roar and Squeaky clattered off in hot pursuit.

As soon as he was out of sight of the crowd, Tanktop opened a flap in his back.

"Ha ha!" he chuckled. "These nails will slow down that robo wreck!"

By the time Squeaky spotted the spiky trap, it was too late.

Luckily, Squeaky was so old that his wheels were made of solid rubber. They didn't burst and he was still in the race.

"I'll show that cheat!" thought Squeaky. He put on a burst of speed. Soon, he'd caught up with Tanktop.

"Let's see you get out of this!" boomed Tanktop, as he opened another compartment.

"Oh no! Oil!" squealed Squeaky.

Squeaky shut his eyes and hoped for the best, as he slithered and slid all over the road.

CRASH!

Squeaky was left battered
and dented, but at least he
was still in one piece.

He tried to get up and
found he couldn't move.
His joints were too stiff.

As he sat there, Squeaky realized what he needed was all around him. Unwinding his hose, he guzzled up every last drop of oil.

SLURP!

Soon, Squeaky was back on his rival's tail. Tanktop was running out of power fast.

But Tanktop still had one trick up his sleeve
– his telescopic arms. He reached out to
Squeaky's front wheel and undid the screw.

Sparks flew through
the air as Squeaky's
wheel bounced past
Tanktop. In seconds,
Squeaky had ground
to a halt.

As the crowd came back into view, Tanktop used the last of his power to roar across the finishing line. "Ha ha, I've won!" he cried.

FLASH!

Tanktop was already boasting to the crowds as poor old Squeaky was carried across the line.

"Congratulations!" cried the judge as he shook Squeaky by the hand.

"Well, I suppose I almost won," Squeaky sniffed, sadly.

"Not almost," said the judge. "You **did** win. Look!"

He showed Squeaky and Tanktop the photograph taken at the finishing line.

"Your wheel crossed the line a second before Tanktop. That makes you the winner!"

Squeaky clunked with delight, the crowd cheered and Tanktop blew a fuse.

The bed monster's secret

Gggrhh

Gggrhh

Ben Boggle lay awake in a cold sweat. How could he sleep with a monster under his bed?

Every evening it was the same story. As soon as Ben switched off his bedside light, the monster woke with a snort.

Grrrgggh
Gruggluggle

All through the night, the creature gurgled and growled in the shadows.

Ben had never dared to look under his bed.
He was too terrified of what he might see.
   Perhaps the monster
had ten eyes...

or long, slimy tentacles...

or huge, sharp teeth...

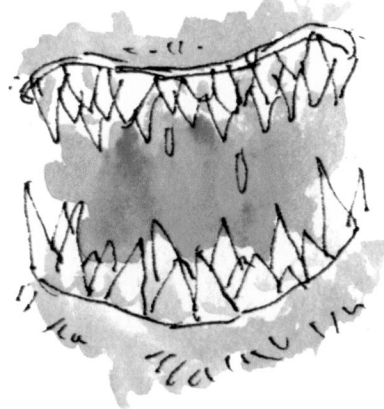

or all of these!

At school, Ben could hardly keep his eyes open.

"Wake up, Ben Boggle!" yelled his teacher.

"That's the third time this week you've fallen asleep in class." Mr. Grizzle liked people to be awake in his mathematics lessons.

Even when he was wide awake, Ben was hopeless with numbers. When he felt sleepy, they were even more difficult.

"Get to bed earlier, young man," said Mr. Grizzle, in a stern voice.

Unless Ben could get rid of the monster, Mr. Grizzle would be shouting at him every day.

Tired and worried, Ben was walking home
when he spotted something in a shop window.

"Maybe that book has something about bed
monsters," Ben thought. He dashed inside.

As soon as he got home, Ben read the book from cover to cover. But there was no mention of monsters under the bed.

"What a waste of money," thought Ben. Then he had an idea. Perhaps the book could help him after all...

Ben decided to build a monster trap. He raided the chocolate chip cookie jar and took a net from his dad's fishing box. In no time at all, his trap was ready.

That night, he climbed into bed, switched off the light and waited.

At first, Ben's room was spookily silent. Then he heard a crunching, munching sound followed by a whoosh. His monster trap had worked!

Nervously, Ben crept over to the net. But nothing could have prepared him for what happened next...

"Please don't hurt me," squeaked a tiny voice. The smallest monster in the world was tangled in the net.

"I can't believe I was scared of you," cried Ben. "I know," the monster said sadly. "I'm too small to scare anyone. That's why I hid under your bed. I didn't want you to see me."

"I'm the most useless monster alive," she wailed and started to sob.

The monster sniffed. "It's impossible to scare people when you only weigh fifteen ounces," she said. "I mean, that's less than half a kilo."

"Is it really?" said Ben.

"Oh yes," replied the monster. "I may be small, but I'm not stupid."

This gave Ben such a great idea that he grinned all night, even in his sleep.

He was still grinning the next day at school as Mr. Grizzle began the lesson.

"Ben Boggle," barked Mr. Grizzle. "What is nine times eight?"

"Seventy two," said Ben, confidently.

Mr. Grizzle couldn't believe his ears. "Oh, that's correct," he said, shakily. He asked Ben problem after problem. Ben answered every one correctly.

Mr. Grizzle was amazed.

"Well done, Ben," he said. "What an astonishing improvement!"

Luckily, no one but Ben had heard the tiny voice whispering the answers.

Ben smiled to himself. Mathematics is a lot easier when you have a monster in your pocket.

Robert Louis Stevenson

Robert Louis Stevenson was born in Scotland in 1850. He is most famous for adventure stories such as *Treasure Island* and *Kidnapped*, and stories of fantastical events such as *The Strange Case of Dr. Jekyll and Mr. Hyde*. He also wrote some well-known poetry for children.

He suffered from tuberculosis and spent a lot of his life in warmer countries for the good of his health. Many of his stories are about exciting journeys and faraway lands, inspired by his travels. He died suddenly in 1894.

Hans Christian Andersen

Hans Christian Andersen was born in a little town in Denmark called Odense, in 1805. His father was a shoemaker and his mother was a washerwoman, and they were very poor.

In fact, his childhood sounds very much like the beginning of a fairy tale, and just as in a fairy tale, Hans left home to seek his fortune when he was still a young boy. At first, he longed to become a famous actor, dancer or singer, but then he discovered his true purpose in life: writing.

Hans was inspired by the stories he heard in Odense as a child, where the old women still told traditional tales and half-believed them, too. He wrote fairy tales based on these stories and became famous all over the world. He died in 1875.

Jacob and Wilhelm Grimm

Jacob and Wilhelm Grimm were brothers who lived in Germany in the early 1800s. They journeyed from village to village in the German countryside, collecting fairy tales. The Grimms published hundreds of these stories during their lifetime, gathering them into large volumes of tales. Wilhelm died in 1858 and his elder brother Jacob died in 1863. Their stories have been told time and again all over the world.

Arthurian legends

Sir Gawain and the Green Knight and *The tale of the kitchen knight* are both set in the legendary court of King Arthur. Arthur may or may not have existed, but legends about the king have been popular ever since medieval times. Stories tell that King Arthur ruled over all of England, with his beautiful wife Guinevere by his side and a band of brave knights at his command. He was advised by a wise and mysterious old wizard named Merlin.

The Nutcracker

The Nutcracker was written by a German writer and composer named E.T.A. Hoffman in 1816. Later, it was adapted by Alexander Dumas, a French writer who also wrote *The Three Musketeers*. In 1892, a Russian composer named Tchaikovsky turned the version by Dumas into a ballet, which is now performed all over the world.

Edited by Lesley Sims and Rachel Firth
Designed by Helen Lee and Tom Lolande
Additional designs by Louise Flutter
Cover and additional illustrations by Anna Luraschi
Digital manipulation by Nick Wakeford
and Mike Wheatley